THE KEY GAME

THE KEY GAME

DON JAMES

CUTTING EDGE

ISBN-13: 978-1-970848-15-1

Published by
Cutting Edge Books
PO Box 8212
Calabasas, CA 91372
www.cuttingedgebooks.com

PART I

THE PLAYER

CHAPTER ONE

In some ways, she thought, it was like the irrevocable losing of one's virginity. In one moment of a day or night you were a virgin, and in the next you were not. It could take only that long, those few seconds, to destroy something that had been carefully preserved for years.

"And being unfaithful to Webster for the first time will be something like that," she told herself. "Like losing my virginity."

Yet there was a difference. Perhaps with some women there would not be quite so much difference; the women who first knew sex on the wedding night, after the careful preparations, the bathing, the special nightgown, the subtleties of perfume and powder, and the careful preparation of the female body for exhibition and love.

"It didn't happen that way for me," she thought with a wry smile, remembering the back seat of Web's car, the smell of spring in the night air, the awkwardness of a garter belt and rayon fabric, the fumbling in the dark, and the sudden, sharp pain.

That was what made the difference. She had prepared herself for adultery with the same meticulous care that other girls and women prepared themselves for the initiation of the marriage bed.

Now she drove gracefully and skillfully through traffic, pacing the convertible to the changing lights. Men who passed her in cars glanced at her in quick appreciation of the yellow hair that gleamed in the summer sun, the small and pretty face, and the poise of self-confidence that was an invisible, disdaining rebuff to those glances.

Her name was Sarah Emmlin. She was thirty-four years old. She was married to Webster Emmlin, four years her senior, and they had no children. Her husband was an advertising account executive for a local agency, and until their marriage—six years before this summer—Sarah had written copy in the same agency. She had resigned her job shortly before the marriage.

Undoubtedly some of the men who glanced at her on the highway that hot afternoon wondered about her; wondered, perhaps, where she was going, and how it would be for a man to have a woman like this one.

The wedding band and engagement ring on her left hand caught and reflected sunlight occasionally as a gentle reminder, to those who noticed, that this was a married woman who probably was concerned with domestic affairs, her husband, and possibly children. She was one of millions who somehow manage to reflect the mold typified by advertisements in consumer magazines; the four-color, beautifully executed paragons of The American Way of Life.

To a degree Sarah Emmlin actually was a part of this socio-economic regimentation of the nation's womanhood. Her home, in the suburbs of Douglas City in the Pacific Northwest, was well equipped with most of the labor-saving devices, most of them bought—despite Webster's fairly adequate salary—on the installment plan.

The car she owned was three years old and was the second of two cars that they owned, both in the "low price field." Lately they had talked about a small compact car for a third vehicle, but had not quite made up their minds to buy one.

The shoes she wore were nationally advertised, the dress was a "name" dress, the brassiere was sold in large quantities and was expensively advertised in print and in TV spots. She wore no hose over her golden tan legs, and her panties would not have been found originally in the less expensive stores. They were lacy and diaphanous. Putting them on this day had awakened an odd excitement of guilt in her.

The guilt and excitement made her fight a little to maintain the composure that she displayed to those who glanced at her in the passing traffic. Actually she was excited and frightened and worried. She had a deep urgency to turn the car back toward her home.

She gripped the car wheel more firmly and reminded herself that the issue really had not been decided just this day ... but weeks or even months before. What was going to happen in the next hour had become inevitable.

She told herself that she would never again know peace of mind until it *had* happened, yet she was almost sick with a nagging fright that she might never find that peace of mind again after it did happen. But she was prepared and she told herself that she must go through with it.

So carefully and deliberately prepared! she thought. Even assignation had its moments of practicality. The diaphanous panties, the new bra, and the summer dress were all carefully selected with a knowledge that probably never would have guided the virgin bride's selections.

For one thing, she knew more about a man's likes and dislikes in the matters of making love than would the neophyte; the places to touch with perfume, the subtlety of fragrant powder, and the erotic significance of black lace and silk. Too, she had dealt efficiently and almost routinely with the problem of contraception before she had dressed.

So she was prepared and dressed and driving to her first assignation. She glanced at a highway sign and realized that her turn-off was only a few miles down the highway. Suddenly all the virtuous years assembled into the weight of conscience and guilt. The solid Presbyterian beliefs and background of her family gathered forces to caution her. Her adult years of comprehension and education and mental adjustment delineated her behavior in her own eyes and she recognized what she was doing.

Very deliberately she thought about Webster, her husband, and it was at that moment that the battle was joined and lost.

She could not picture Webster's eyes accusing her. She could only remember his eyes as he looked away evasively when she had walked into the room and found him with Agnes Aiten.

She could not visualize Webster as the outraged husband, but only as the errant husband who had been discovered. She could not think of Webster with the loyalty and warmth she once had known, but now only with an empty anger and disillusionment and the sense of having lost something that once had been of value to her. The change in feeling toward him had become strong and significant, even in small things. *I usually think of him now as Webster—not as Web,* she thought.

Of course there had been the subsequent talks and scenes and efforts to forgive; the reconciliations and assurances. None of it had been enough. Nothing had worked out right about it. So now, as she approached the turn-off, the battle was joined and lost.

She slowed the car for the turn-off and then drove up a winding road toward the summit of a mountain. Carl Trojan was waiting in his car.

He waved and immediately took off from his parking place beside the road. She followed his car as he left the road for an unpaved driveway that took them through trees and heavy brush. He stopped his car at a small summerhouse. She parked behind him and got out of the convertible.

"I wasn't certain you'd come," he smiled.

"Neither was I," she admitted.

He nodded solemnly and looked down at her from his tallness; a well-proportioned, middle-aged man with light brown eyes, very tanned skin and a pleasant smile. He was a building contractor; not affluent in the sense of great suburban or city developments, but capable and trustworthy within the limitations of the business that he sought and enjoyed; the smaller homes, the smaller developments, and the occasional small industrial or office building.

His wife, Lillian, continually and insistently was busy with secondary civic affairs, clubs and periodic attempts to combat the inroads that approaching middle age were making upon her body.

Once she had possessed the good looks that go well with the athletic girl who excels on the tennis court, the golf course and in the swimming pool. Now she was beginning to show the lack of exercise with an increase in weight and a certain looseness of body tone.

If Sarah Emmlin had liked her better, she might have harbored a depth of guilt about betraying a woman friend. As a matter of fact, Sarah vaguely sensed that Lillian Trojan would not particularly care if she were to know about the clandestine meeting at the deserted summer home in the mountains.

"I opened the windows and aired out the place," Carl Trojan said. "I even dusted a little. And compared with the heat out here, it's reasonably cool inside."

She nodded silently and they walked to the small house. He opened the door and they stepped inside. He closed the door after them and she heard the spring lock snap into place.

The sound was a sharp reminder that now they were alone and locked away from the world. There was a finality in the sound; a cutting of bonds. Suddenly she knew that she had to stop thinking if she wanted to go through with it. She had to run away from logic and morals and conventions and doubts. She must let her body lead the way.

She turned and pressed against him, blindly, with closed eyes. She lifted her face and felt his kiss—soft, gentle and tentative at first, then demanding and open. Her body responded as she knew it could. She felt her hunger rise and become as demanding as his. She moved against him, shamelessly, inviting and offering.

"Please hurry," she whispered. "Please ... now ... while I'm ready. I don't want to think ..."

He picked her up and carried her into the bedroom. Then it was not as she had planned it, nor as she supposed it might be. So much of the careful preparation was wasted in their hard, relentless haste—a haste marked by clothing carelessly dropped on the floor, the urgent wedding of bodies upon the bed, the half-spoken words of endearment, the exclamations and soft cries of pleasure in the taking and reception: then only the hard breathing, the gentle moaning as the abandoned, soaring cadence of their lovemaking carried them to a sudden, gasping climax.

Afterward, she stared at the ceiling of the room, listening to the rhythm of his breathing and the summer sounds beyond the open window.

"Was it all right?" Trojan asked softly.

"You know it was," she said.

"It was so quick. I wasn't certain."

"Do we have to be clinical?"

"No. I just wanted to be sure. You're wonderful. I wanted it to be as good for you as it was for me. I was afraid I was too quick."

She shut her eyes and thought about it as he wanted her to do. Now that it had happened, she tried to gauge how it had been and what it had done to her.

At last she said, "It was good, if that's the word. It was sudden and explosive and complete. Before I knew what was happening. And now I feel spent ... completely spent. Is that what you want to know?" You could so easily hurt a man; the sensitive, proud men who were so sensitive about their sexual abilities. "Yes, it was good."

He seemed to be satisfied with her answer. He sighed.

"Sleepy?" he asked lazily.

"Yes." She smiled and turned her head so that she could look at him. She was being honest. She was spent and momentarily satisfied and she was sleepy. "Do we have time?"

"Of course. A cigarette first?"

"No. You have one if you like."

"I think not." He had turned to look at her, and they were both relaxed and sprawled out on the bed. The room was warm, almost hot.

He rested on one side so that he could look at her. One of his lean, strong hands cupped a breast.

"You have a lovely body," he said. "A girl's body with a woman's response."

She searched his eyes, her head still turned on the pillow, her body quiet under his hand.

She was wholly conscious of herself, in small detail, in physical presence. She knew that her lips were swollen and bruised from his mouth. She still felt his weight upon her breasts. She was conscious of the dampness of the sheet beneath her.

These things were virtually the same under any of the circumstances of habitual love-making, she thought. Nothing was changed about some of the details. A man had taken her and enjoyed her and certain incidental conditions were the same; the bruised lips, the conscious remembrance of weight upon breasts, the feel of having been possessed and used.

Thoughtfully she said, "You're the only man other than Webster who has ever touched my bare breasts. The only man other than Webster who has ever had me."

"I believe you," he said simply.

She looked at this thin, strong mouth, at the firm masculine throat, at the lean, muscled hardness of his shoulders and chest.

Abruptly she rolled to face him and came close against him so that his arms came around her and held her. Their lips met and clung and she shut her eyes.

There's a difference, she thought. *How terrible to compare! How shameless! How natural! Webster is heavier, softer—almost too soft. Carl is sinewy and hard muscled and active and vital. He feels different against me. His arms feel different. Probably there was a difference in the lovemaking, only it was too intense, violent, breathless and blinding. There's nothing else to remember. No details.*

She shut her eyes and it was as if the lights had been turned out. When she awakened she knew that he had pulled her a little closer to him and as she opened her eyes he kissed her.

"I want to make love again," he said.

This time they sought the more deliberate nuances of lovemaking; the questing hands and lips, the awakening, and heightening, and soaring of desires toward a planned and certain goal. Deliberately and almost breathlessly they built the cadence of possession and submission into their own perfection. His hands and mouth were eager and wanton in their love play upon her breasts and gradually a wild, soaring sensation flowed through her loins and up and down her limbs.

"Oh, yes ... yes ... yes ..." she whispered.

"Now!" he said. *"Now!"*

Then lassitude was deliciously heavy as she lay free of him, arms out, eyes shut, lips parted, legs spread carelessly. Now she could compare and recognize the difference, for Webster never had taken her as completely as Carl had taken her. Or was it the circumstance that added to the excitement? Did deep guilt and a taste of the forbidden lend flavor to the act?

They drowsed for ten minutes, neither speaking, their hands touching, satiation a mutual and satisfactory thing.

"We'd better go," she finally said.

"Yes." He paused and then added, "Do I have to tell you?"

"What?"

"How good you are for me? Never anyone else … never."

"I'm glad I pleased you."

They dressed quickly, both trying to disguise the sudden and unexplained modesty that seemed to take them; the strange modesty of lovers who have just discovered one another, and tasted, and are calmed, and preoccupied with the mundane task of clothing their bodies again.

They were dressed and she shook her head when he offered her a cigarette. They walked into the small living room of the cottage and he indicated a sofa.

"Until I've finished my smoke," he suggested.

She sat at the opposite end of the sofa and watched him smoke. He was frowning a little.

"I don't like questions afterward," he said. "It's none of my business. I want you and need you as you are. I'm glad I was the first—other than Web. But I've wondered. I mean the parties."

"The key game?" she smiled.

He shrugged a little. "Most of the crowd play it—except Lillian and me, and I've noticed that you have always found a reason to leave when the idea came up. It's been pretty well accepted that you—well …"

"You wonder what happened today when I've refused before?"

He smiled. "Something like that."

"Is that all this afternoon meant to you? Another woman? Like a night of the key game?" she asked, realizing that sudden anger edged her voice.

"You know better than that. You know how it is with us now. I suppose that sex can be good almost any time as long as the people like one another. But when there's something extra—and there is with us—it's better than anything else in sex can be. We learned that today, didn't we?"

"Then why are you asking questions?"

"Don't be angry. I'm not prying. I'm simply in love with you. I want to know about you."

"Love? Is that the something extra between us?"

"*I* think so, Sarah. How else could I explain wanting you so desperately for so long—needing you so much?

Now we're making talk, she thought. *And I don't know what I really mean. I don't know what he means. We went to bed together and we were a man and a woman together. I suppose—under these conditions—we have to rationalize it now. Maybe I do love him. Maybe he loves me.*

"Listen to me, Carl," she said thoughtfully. "I want to explain it to myself, if I can. How it happened, I mean."

"Can you?"

"I think so. Beginning with the way you've looked at me ever since we met two years ago, and at the parties, and when we danced together, and finally the night at the Halbruths when you kissed me. Do you remember?"

"Of course I remember. I'd been wanting to kiss you since the first time I met you. And that night we'd all had enough drinks so that I could be a little more daring—and you, too, perhaps."

"Perhaps."

"And it began then?"

"It was the first time I was conscious of wanting some man other than Web. I shouldn't tell you that, but I want to understand it myself."

"The blueprint of how it was built," he smiled. "And that's all there is to understand. It was mutual. Finally it has happened."

"Yes," she said pensively. "It's happened. It's started—and now I'm afraid."

"Of what?"

She smiled thinly. "Me, I guess. I don't feel guilty. I don't feel ... I guess the word is *whorish*. It was too easy, and now it's too easy to accept since it's happened."

He frowned. "I don't want you to think that it's nothing more than a quick roll in the hay to me," he said, a little sharply. "Not you. Never *you*."

She shook her head and smiled again. "Maybe I'm going to become a loose woman, Carl."

"I think not."

"Maybe I'll try the key game. I know that Web is dying to play it—in the open, that is. I think his whole relationship with women all his life has been a sort of key game."

"I don't think I'd like you to play the key game."

"You don't have much to say about it, Carl."

"Certainly I do! After this afternoon. Because of what's between us."

"That's your interpretation. I don't know what's between us, Carl. Truly I don't. I'm not in love. At least, I don't believe I am. Can't we just accept it for what it was and is?"

"I don't understand you!"

"Don't try, Carl. Please don't. Now ... let's go. It's getting late."

"Not until we've talked this out and—"

"It's no use. There's nothing to talk out. You enjoyed the afternoon, didn't you?"

"That isn't the point. I mean about you and me—"

She stood and started for the door.

"There'll probably be other afternoons," she said. "I enjoyed it, too. Very much, Carl. Very much. But I can't chart the rest of my life from what happened this afternoon."

He caught her at the door and held the doorknob as he looked down at her.

"You know," he mused thoughtfully, "you could be a ... a ..." He hesitated and shook his head in exasperation.

"Bitch is the word," she said. She laughed and turned the knob beneath the pressure of his hand and pulled the door open.

Driving home alone, Sarah swung away from the arterial highway and stayed on the back roads. It was, she thought, a time for introspection. What had happened during the afternoon was a definite milestone of a sort. All through your life you had milestones. Not everyone had the same ones, but many did; the women had their mutual milestones and the men had theirs.

You could almost generalize, Sarah told herself. The most simple milestones for a woman possibly were birth, marriage, childbirth and death. But a great deal could be filled in between the milestones. All the "firsts." The first high heels, the first date, the first kiss, the first dance, the first graduation, the first love affair, the first time with a man, the first quarrel, the first anniversary, the first child, the first death of a dear one. It went on and on with firsts, and a great many women kept track of the firsts in a private mental datebook of occasions, memories, anniversaries, joys, sorrows and frustrations.

So, she thought, another first. The first time unfaithful. The first time with another man. The first time it was as good as it had been. Even during the honeymoon and the first years when sex still was important between Web and her there had been nothing as good for her as it had been this afternoon between Carl Trojan and her.

There had been another first, she thought. A strange, long-ago first time when she was thirteen and her brother, Harold, was a year older.

People often remarked how "close" the brother and sister were. There was virtually no bickering between the two; rather, there existed a deep understanding and sibling affection that removed them into a world peopled by their own imaginations, shared secrets and mutual impulses.

Adolescence and adulthood were to change greatly the bond between the brother and sister. When Sarah was seven she firmly had proclaimed that she intended to marry her brother when she grew up. Harold, at eight, had accepted her plans.

Now Harold was married and living in New York. The brother and sister seldom met, but letters were frequent and the bond still was strong.

And there was the rainy afternoon when she was thirteen and they were in the attic of the old house on Elm Street; the secret Harold had just learned about men and women; the four-letter word another boy had used in describing the act.

What happened that afternoon between brother and sister was immature, inexperienced and incomplete. But Sarah was budding rapidly. There was much more than a mere suggestion of breasts at thirteen, and there were strange emotions and sensations aroused by the fumbling and touching, and even in the failure.

Harold was frightened when she cried, the tears squeezing from tightly closed eyes.

"Don't cry, Sarah. Please don't cry. We won't do it."

So nothing more happened. She put on her panties and they never spoke again of the experiment, but they kissed frequently later on in a half-teasing, half-experimental way.

And if the afternoon was not successful in one way, it served to awaken Sarah to the possibilities and mysteries of sex. She listened and sometimes she talked with other girls. As she grew into the fullness of adolescence her body began to assert its restless impulses and sometimes in the dark of a restless night she touched herself intimately and soon learned what that searching exploration of her body could do to her feelings.

Later, when she was at the university, she occasionally had strange, erotic dreams in which her brother usually was a component. She awakened from these dreams in great restlessness and with a disturbed feeling of guilt, realizing that in her dreams—and sometimes when she was not dreaming—the dream or the thought of Harold awakened her erotically.

The confusions of childhood, the frustrations and mysteries of adolescence became somewhat cleared in the university. From her courses in psychology and pertinent reading she understood her own relationship to her brother and the overtones that might be sexual in substance. She learned that such feelings between brother and sister were not wholly uncommon. She learned that incest was ancient; that the relationship between men and women could be based upon elemental urges.

Essentially her family background had been middle-class small town. Her father, Charles Bruhand, had been an accountant for a small lumber mill. Her mother, Laura, of Scottish descent, had been a staunch Presbyterian. Sarah and Harold had been reared in an atmosphere of respectability and commonplace planning.

Charles Bruhand and his wife carefully saved for the education of their children. Harold was caught late in the surge of

World War II, served briefly in the Pacific area, and returned to complete his schooling. Sarah finished high school during the war years and continued on to the university.

She turned to journalism in school because she liked words and had visions of eventually becoming a writer. After graduation she discovered that jobs on newspapers were difficult to find. Finally she found a job writing advertising copy—a job that was to lead her to the agency where she met Webster Emmlin, recently returned from war, and beginning his career as a junior account executive.

Web Emmlin took her by storm. He flattered her, courted her and finally seduced her. The seduction came only after he had proposed marriage after a long and fruitless campaign to break down the safeguards carefully placed by her family background, and disturbingly confused by the transgressions with her brother, both physical and mental.

As Sarah drove home now, after her most serious transgression, she abruptly realized that she could now view herself with the greatest clarity and objectivity she ever had known.

"It's always been mixed up for me," she told herself. "Always. Maybe it began with Harold. Maybe Web happened because he's so much like Harold in appearance and in some of the things he does. Tell yourself the truths now—all the truths you never wanted to admit before. The most secret and dark truths. The times you pretended."

Even alone, driving the back road, years later, she almost felt a blush as she deliberately remembered things she had tried to bury in her mind.

There was the night when she and Web had gone to San Francisco where they had met Harold and his new wife. They had gone to a nightclub and there had been a small reunion dinner, drinks and dancing. Harold had danced with her and it was different. Even as they danced she thought how it must be for him and a wife, with this girl, Margaret, whom he had so recently married.

She, herself, now knew how it was with a man—fully and in completion of what she and Harold had failed to consummate when they were younger. She shut her eyes and chided herself for her thoughts. Deliberately she tried to think of other things. The drinks were betraying her and with her eyes shut she was almost hypnotically conscious of Harold's masculine body and the rhythm of their movements. They always had danced well together. They did most things well together; the brother-and-sister closeness.

All through the evening she kept their conversation on a safe plateau. Carefully she extended her display of family affection to her new sister-in-law. Carefully she maintained a half-bantering, affectionate attitude toward her brother.

It was a pleasant, satisfying and mildly exciting evening. But afterward, in the insinuating unfamiliarity of the hotel room, Webster had wanted to make love and she had accepted him in the dark room with the night sounds of San Francisco seemingly close under their hotel window, and her usual inhibitions dropping away, one by one, under the numbing release of too many drinks and Web's mounting excitement.

She had let her body surrender. Her imagination broke loose and escaped into unexplored paths of the subconscious.

Almost jealously, and in guilt, she wondered if her brother was now with the girl he had married in this age-old embrace of the marriage bed. She wondered how it was with them. She wondered how it would be with Harold.

Suddenly she was more excited than she ever had been. *Harold,* she thought. *It could have been Harold once long ago. If we had been older and knew. Harold doing this ...*

Then she abandoned herself to the awesome and overpowering wave of sensation that was engulfing her and when she cried out in her relief she almost moaned *"Harold!"* She caught the word at her lips, almost subconsciously, and forced her intensity of release to die quickly.

"Christ!" Webster moaned. "You were never like that before! What happened?" He moved again and was heavy upon her. "What happened? Maybe we'd better try drinks now and then!" He laughed softly and a little smugly. "Don't tell me *that* wasn't good, baby! That was *it!* Like never before!"

She listened to him and let him believe what he wished. Her guilt swept over her in a wave of revulsion that almost made her ill. Then—only once—she said it silently to herself, and she never had dared even to think about it again because she had buried it so very deeply in a grave of guilt.

But in those few seconds of spent moments she silently said it to herself: *It was good because I imagined you were Harold!*

Even now as she allowed herself to dredge up the memory from the past she felt her guilt and shame. Despite what she had read and studied and learned, she had been almost physically guilty of incest, and certainly she had been mentally guilty that night in San Francisco.

She stepped on the gas and the car sped forward. She didn't want to think about it now. She had another transgression to think about. She wanted to get home and take a shower before Webster came home from the agency.

CHAPTER TWO

At almost the exact moment that Sarah Emmlin was sitting on a sofa talking with the man who had just made love to her, Webster Emmlin, her husband, was sitting at his desk scowling at a television story board for one of the clients served by Jorsen, Lanner and Associates, Advertising.

At thirty-eight he looked fit, although a trifle heavy for his slightly under six feet of height. His brown hair was cut in the approved shortness currently favored by young executives. When he worked with copy he wore glasses with heavy black frames, also favored in the smarter offices.

He glanced up from the story board and across the desk at the thirtyish woman who watched him intently. She was a little too thin, but she was pretty with smooth blond hair, blue eyes—as blue as Emmlin's, and strangely like them in a certain boldness of glance—and beneath the smartly tailored blouse and close-fitting skirt was a trim figure.

Agnes Aiten, thirty-two and unmarried, headed the TV-radio department in the agency. She was creative, resourceful and competent. She had been sleeping occasionally with Web Emmlin for about eight years. She had slept with him before Sarah Bruhand had come to work for the agency. After marriage had begun to bore Web, she had slept with him again. Indeed, she and Web had been discovered at an inopportune moment by Sarah at an agency party that had gotten a little out of hand and when Web discovered the back bedroom in Tad Lanner's rambling house.

Agnes still cringed at the thought of that moment. It had begun with too many drinks, as usual, and somehow there was a great amount of milling around and lights going out here and there. Most of the group preferred the living room, patio or swimming pool that was Lanner's enthusiasm.

The party was in celebration of the acquisition of a half-million-dollar utilities account and it had grown from a small beginning at the agency to large proportions when congratulatory television, radio, newspaper and other media "reps" appeared; when suppliers dropped in to congratulate the agency people; and when the agency men called their wives and told them to forget dinner because there was going to be a party at Lanner's. Sarah had come, of course.

Agnes vividly remembered the moment when someone turned on the light in the bedroom where she and Web had found privacy; of looking toward the doorway where Sarah Emmlin stood, eyes wide, face frozen in an expression of shock.

Sarah turned and left them. Web swore a soft oath and they got up from the bed and arranged their clothing in silence.

"Look, Aggie," he started to say, but she put a hand to his mouth.

"Don't say anything," she said. "Let's just get out of here. I'll go home. I don't know how you're going to handle it, but I don't want to see her again—ever, if that's possible."

"It isn't. I don't know what she'll do."

Web was soon to find out what Sarah intended to do, and he also was to learn that Sarah was not certain how far things had progressed between Aggie and him. She told him that night when they were home.

Standing in their bedroom, her back to him as she unfastened a pearl necklace, she voiced it simply and decisively.

"I don't know how far things have gone between you two," she said, speaking to him in the mirror. "I wasn't certain even when I turned on the light. But I do know that it was far enough for me to make up my mind."

"To do what?"

"To give you one more chance."

"It wasn't that serious," he said.

"Maybe. I don't know. I never was certain how it was between you and Aggie before I went to work at the agency. I heard things. For one thing, that you were sleeping together for quite a while. I overlooked that. It was before we met. But I won't overlook it if it's going on now."

"Just because we were—"

"I know," she interrupted. "Everyone had too much to drink. It was one of those parties. So we'll skip it for a while. Only ..." She hesitated thoughtfully and turned away from the mirror to face him.

"What?" he prompted.

"*I'm* sleeping alone until I decide. Is that clear?"

For the first time his anger came to the surface. "What's different about that?" he snapped. "For the last year."

"You can't say that I haven't granted you—as they used to say—your 'marital rights,'" she replied evenly.

"Is that what you call it? That cold pretense? That indifferent permission? That unresponsive accommodation you grant me on rare occasions because it's your duty?"

"Maybe we'd better talk divorce," she retorted, but even as she spoke the words, her eyes looked away from his face. She knew as well as he that her response in bed had been anything but enthusiastic.

"Perhaps we should," he said.

They continued to undress in silence. They went to bed without speaking again and in the morning neither broached the subject.

They had twin beds and there was no occasion to test the validity of her determination to end their physical relationship. So it had continued for six months. The subject of divorce remained unmentioned and there was a strange truce between them.

Nor had there been an active continuance of the relationship between Agnes Aiten and him after that night. For one thing, the incident had caused Agnes to withdraw into a protective shell. She obviously was embarrassed and guilt-stricken. She avoided him at the agency, restricting her relations with him to the business of advertising, as at this moment.

"It's a good spot," he said, indicating the story board.

"Does the client have to okay it?"

"Yes. I'll show it in the morning. I'll need production costs, too."

She nodded and stood up, ready to leave his office, but he was ahead of her, stepping to the door before she did and closing it firmly. He leaned back against the door and looked down into her blue eyes, thinking how often he had looked into the pretty face against a pillow, with the eyes closed, the mouth parted and waiting. The thought excited him.

"It's been a long time," he said.

She smiled thinly. "And it's going to be longer, Web. It's finished."

"I don't think so."

He put his hands on her shoulders and drew her toward him, securing their privacy with the weight of his body against the door that opened into the hallway serving as the traffic core of the agency.

She resisted his movement, but he was firm and when he had pulled her close against him, his hands slid down her body and he clasped them at the small of her back so that their bodies were pressed tightly together. She stared into his face.

"Really, Web," she said. "It's no good."

"What do you mean, no good?" he smiled. The firmness of her slim body had awakened him. He bent to kiss her and she turned her head away.

"No," she said. "I mean it, Web. No more."

His hands left the small of her back in a quick movement so that he held her head and turned her face to him. He covered her lips hard and hungrily. For a few seconds she struggled against his strength and her lips were tight and unresponsive, and then she was suddenly loose and receptive. Her mouth opened to him and their kiss became deep and intense. Their bodies moved, writhing sinuously back and forth.

He released her after a few moments and she stepped back, breathing a little hard, her eyes sultry, her mouth wet and swollen.

"You bastard," she said.

Deliberately he reached forward and cupped her breasts. She remained motionless, still breathing hard. Then she came into his arms again, pressing hard against him, her mouth eager, her arms around his neck as he strained her to him.

"Can you leave early?" he asked softly.

"Yes. Can you?"

"About four. Your place?"

"Yes. I hate you—but yes."

She stepped away from him and took a deep breath. She put her hands to her hair and went to a small closet that concealed a mirror and washbasin. She opened the closet door and inspected her hair and lipstick.

Web returned to his desk and carefully wiped his mouth with a tissue from a package in a desk drawer. He glanced down at the story board again.

"This is a hell of a good spot, Aggie," he said. "You're good." He looked up at her and smiled. "At this, too."

She smiled and went to the door.

"We're crazy," she said. "Or I am. Starting it again."

"That's how it is with us, Aggie. I'm that way about you. I always will be."

"It's odd," she said thoughtfully, her hand on the doorknob.

"What?"

"I've never wanted to marry you. Sometimes I wish I'd fall in love with someone. *Really* in love, I mean." She opened the door and went out.

His telephone rang as he watched her leave. He picked up the instrument. A client identified himself and asked for a progress report on a series of magazine ads in preparation.

Web gave a complete, detailed accounting, being careful to inject an undertone of sustained enthusiasm for the ads and the campaign, but even as he talked his mind skipped ahead to later in the afternoon and he visualized Aggie's bedroom and how she would look on the white sheets of her bed.

After he finished talking with the client he closed the door Aggie had left open and returned to his desk. He hoped that he had sounded enthusiastic and confident enough to please the client. This was one of his accounts that was on the shaky side. He couldn't afford trouble in the agency now.

He glanced at his desk calendar to check appointments. He had none for the remainder of the day; none to break with one excuse or another while he went to bed with Aggie in her apartment.

The year on the calendar sheet caught his attention and he realized abruptly that this month marked his ninth year with the agency. Sometimes it didn't seem that he was accomplishing much with the years.

He had been born and reared in Ypsilanti, Michigan. He had gone to war and he had returned unscathed. He had finished his schooling on the West Coast, probably because he had served in the Pacific area and had been stationed on the West Coast long enough to like the change from the Michigan country and seasons.

He had taken the job in the agency upon his graduation, with a half-formed plan of working in a small agency for a time before going East to the more important fields in Chicago and New York.

Somehow the jobs in the East never had developed and he gradually had built himself a routine—a dull routine at times—in the agency. He knew by now that he had shortcomings. He knew that he lacked any unusual creative ability in advertising, but he had a fair talent for servicing an account, of being able to agree with clients, and to make them believe that he was competent and devoted solely to their businesses, each one individually.

He leaned heavily upon the agency's creative and media departments. On occasion he took one of the agency heads with him to sell the more ambitious campaigns. He never had been offered a vice-presidency. He never had been offered a job by another important agency. He had found a fairly safe niche and he stayed in it, not setting the advertising world on fire, not greatly increasing the agency business, but doing an adequate job in holding the accounts to which he was assigned.

His salary was sufficient for his needs, but not large. He shared a yearly bonus with other members of the staff, and he was building a modest reserve in a company retirement fund.

All this had brought him a three-bedroom house in a good neighborhood—purchased on a long-term GI loan—a car for himself and one for his wife. He belonged to a country club, for which the agency picked up the membership tab and some of the expenses (when he entertained clients). He could afford—and bought—good clothes.

Sometimes he wasn't quite certain why he had married Sarah. When she came to work at the agency he already had established a satisfactory relationship with Aggie, who at that time was just embarking on her own career in the copy department.

But Sarah had come to work for Jorsen, Lanner and Associates. She was not too long out of school, and she had a smattering of experience writing fashion copy for a local department store. The agency had hired her to do the same type of copy for the single fashion account that it serviced—a small manufacturer of casuals for women.

He began really to notice her during a three-week period when Aggie was away on vacation. He took Sarah out and it quickly became more than a casual thing.

They went to nightclubs, they danced, they took long drives into the country, they had dinners at small and out-of-the-way places, they swam at the beach, they talked, and they parked in the summer nights and he held her small, beautifully molded body close. They kissed and they continued their talks and comparisons and explorations of one another's background, life, likes, dislikes, beliefs, ambitions. Sometimes, when they had been drinking a little more than usual, they parked and they didn't talk much.

It was on such a night that Sarah kept her eyes shut, and said "No" without meaning it—even as his hands found the firmness of her breasts and the exciting smoothness of her inner thighs; even as she abandoned herself to his deep, breathless kiss and raised herself to let him remove the last barrier of feminine lace and transparency.

She felt her skirt ride high and a hand fumbled between their bodies. For a frantic few seconds she tried to push up and away from him, but now he was over her, forcing apart, probing and demanding without words.

His mouth on hers stifled her last protest. His hands spread beneath her, and suddenly she moaned in pain and fright and pleasure as his driving passion carried him past the final barrier of her resistance and he possessed her fully and completely.

Afterward she wept, and he felt his guilt and confessed his concern over the theft of her virginity.

Several years later he sometimes wondered if it might have been his guilt that eventually brought about the marriage. Certainly there had been three weeks of anxious waiting before they were certain that she was not pregnant, and during the mutual worry and waiting they became close and united in the way of a man and wife.

When Agnes returned she seemed unabashed that he had taken up with the new girl in the agency. Within a week she was dating a space salesman from a newspaper, and later an attorney.

Four years after his marriage to Sarah, Web realized that he was bored with his marriage and his wife—with her predictable conservatism, her failure to excite him, her aloofness to the unusual or unconventional.

The thing with Agnes began again easily and without much ado. They worked late one night and he suggested drinks afterward. Two hours later she invited him into her apartment for a nightcap. They stood in her kitchen with an open bottle of bourbon on a counter top. When they finished their drinks, he took her in his arms and kissed her.

"Let's go to bed," he said. It began as simply as that.

"Why not?" she replied. "I'll hate myself in the morning, but why not?"

They had gone to bed hurriedly and then they had made love leisurely, as it had been before.

From that point on it was almost routine to slip back into the set pattern of their love-making. It continued until the night of the party when Sarah discovered them. Since then Aggie had been as cold to his advances as his wife had become in previous months and years.

By now the normal compulsion of his need was becoming a burden to him. Nor could he successfully conceal his marital unhappiness completely from those who knew him best. To a few he confessed his strained relationship with Sarah.

One of these confidants was Len Vember. Actually Len Vember was much more than a confidant to Web. The big, gray-haired automobile dealer was not only one of Web's most important clients, but Vember and his wife, Maxine, had formed the hard-core group of party enthusiasts who consummated the Saturday night parties with spouse-trading in the form of the "key game."

Web had lunched recently with Vember, had told Vember about Sarah's coolness, and had released a brief diatribe against marriage itself.

In the following days Web remembered details of the ensuing conversation, almost word for word.

"It's common gossip that Sarah surprised you and Aggie at a party the agency was throwing," Vember grinned. "Maybe you ought to give her a good chance to get even."

"Sarah? How?"

"Why don't you suggest the key game to her?"

"To Sarah? The key game? Not her!" Web laughed a little. "Not with her steel-ribbed set of morals, conventions, distastes and fastidious dislike for bedroom games. You know how she's avoided it."

Vember nodded. "I know. She's let us all know what she thought about it. But aren't things changed now?"

"Forget it, Len. Maybe the idea is good—but it wouldn't work with her."

"You're not looking down your nose a little, are you?" Vember chided.

Web swallowed the last of his third luncheon martini. He was drinking too many of them lately. It was part of the frustration pattern.

"Me?" he said quickly. "Hell, no! Len, you know me better than that!"

Actually he was not certain what he did think of the key game. This belonged to the "sophisticated" group headed by Len and Maxine Vember. A half-dozen or so couples were in the group who habitually culminated the larger Saturday night parties with a post-party session of spouse-trading.

Web admitted to himself that when he first learned about the practice he had been shocked but strangely excited by the idea. He and Sarah had stayed later than usual at one of the Saturday night parties at Vembers. Several couples had left and five couples remained.

Drinking had been steady and heavy. Sarah was pressing to go home, but Web had reached the stage where another drink seemed to be imperative.

He had noticed the glances that shuttled between the couples who remained, and several questioning nods toward Sarah and him. Finally Maxine Vember brought Sarah and Web together.

"Do you want to play?" she asked pointedly as several of the husbands threw house keys into the center of the floor.

"Play what?" Web asked.

"The key game. We're quite—shall we say 'progressive' in our thinking. Surely you know about it. The selected circle. You're invited."

Sarah asked cautiously, "You mean *the* key game?"

"Each gal draws a house key—making certain it's not her husband's," Maxine explained. "And then you go home with the man who *didn't* bring you! A temporary new husband for the rest of the night." She smiled and added, "With full marital rights included."

Sarah blushed. She understood completely what was meant. She recently had read about the "key game" in a national magazine.

"I'm afraid not." Her smile was forced. Obviously she was trying to conceal her shock. Maxine was Len's wife and Len was one of Web's clients. She should do nothing to cause trouble between them, despite her sudden disgust and disillusionment about the Vembers and some of the others in the group. She had heard vague references to things happening after the usual parties, but she had assumed they didn't include the key game.

Maxine Vember detected Sarah's shock. "Oh?" she smiled, her eyebrows raising slightly in skepticism. "I thought you'd understand. You and Web seem to be so ... knowledgeable." She smiled at Web.

At that moment—seeing invitation in Maxine Vember's eyes and hearing the slight challenge in her voice—he would have been most willing to play the key game; especially if there was a chance that Maxine Vember would be his partner for the remainder of the night. Besides ... maybe another man would be good for Sarah. Maybe she'd appreciate what she had in him.

His thoughts actually shocked him as he realized, with a small jolt of sobriety, that he was not stricken with jealousy by the thought of someone else enjoying his wife, but rather that the thought awakened a small vicarious excitement that almost frightened him.

Before he could say anything, Sarah recovered her poise and managed to turn aside the suggestion with a logical excuse.

"Oh, I understand the key game," she smiled. Then she lied quite believingly rather than to speak her mind and risk an unpleasantness with one of Web's clients or the client's wife. "But I'm afraid my gynecologist wouldn't approve right now."

"Oh, you're pregnant!" Maxine exclaimed, almost bantering the words.

"No, darling. I said gynecologist—not obstetrician. I'd rather not be specific, so let's just say 'female trouble'?" She smiled brightly at her hostess and then at Web. "Web, we'd better be going. It's so late. It's been a wonderful party, Maxine."

Len Vember had approached the threesome and had heard most of the conversation.

"Sure you won't stay?" he grinned. "We might dispense with some of the rules this once—I mean just the four of us. After all, Maxine and I did start the whole thing. We should be granted initiation privileges once in a while!"

"You're a thoughtful and dear host," Sarah said, attempting the light touch. "I'll forever regret refusing—but the gynecologist …" She smiled again and reached for her husband's hand. "Come on, Web, and stop dreaming."

They managed an exit and in their car Sarah lit a cigarette with trembling fingers.

"I thought I was going to be sick," she said. "Web—did you know about this? The key game?"

"Len mentioned it. Once or twice he asked us to stay on for the fun after the big party, but I didn't think you'd be interested."

"Meaning you would?" she snapped.

He tried to laugh it off. "A man's a man! Not really, Sarah. No."

"You'd share me with another man?"

"Look … you're trying to make something out of nothing. I didn't say I wanted to stay. I didn't say anything about it. Let's not make a big deal out of something that doesn't exist. If they want to play adultery and musical beds that's up to them. They're old enough. They know what they're doing."

"But it's so—*repulsive.*"

"What? The adultery or the sex?"

"Meaning?"

"Well, you're not exactly the hottest thing in the hay, you know."

"Let's not start *that* again. You and sex. Is that all you ever think about?"

"Why are *you* getting so steamed up?" he demanded. "It's part of marriage, isn't it?"

"Oh, shut up," Sarah said wearily, crowding back into her corner of the car seat and staring at the street ahead of them. "Just shut up, Web. You'd never understand. You never have. You never will."

"I've tried."

"Suggesting that I see a psychiatrist? Accusing me of being frigid? That song and dance about understanding that I might have a mental block—a phobia—an obsession about sex? You understand just as long as you think it'll net *you* something. If a psychiatrist might tell me to have intercourse with you more often. Or if they could give me something to make it better for you. As you like to say—hot in the hay. God! I hate that expression! And what you *don't* understand is simply that I don't like it any more the way it is. You don't—oh, what's the use!"

"Blaming me?"

"You *could* be to blame."

"All right. Skip it."

That was the last time the key game was discussed. Like any other subject that concerned sex, Sarah carefully skirted the fringes of discussion.

Occasionally and almost upon demand—sometimes Web bitterly thought about it as sex contracted by a marriage vow and payable upon demand—she allowed him to come to her bed. It was brief and unsatisfactory; devoid of response and solely functional; without culmination for Sarah, and a mechanical release for Web.

For a short time after their marriage it had been different, and perhaps for a time before their marriage when he was initiating Sarah into the mysteries of sex. But it had ebbed away into almost nothing for her and a biting frustration for him.

If he was to blame for some of the dissatisfaction, he rationalized the blame by asserting that she refused to approach their marital relations with a willingness and freedom from inhibition. For her part, she apparently sought the esoteric rather than the erotic; the aesthetic rather than the athletic in the confines of the marital bed.

Her discovery of his dalliance with Aggie had been the final breaking point and since that time he had been denied even the functional acquiescence he had managed to obtain for several years.

These thoughts held his attention for the brief remainder of the afternoon while he anxiously awaited the time he would leave to be with Aggie in her apartment.

The telephone rang as he was about to leave and he recognized Len Vember's voice.

"Those TV spots brought us floor traffic," Vember told him. "Let's try some more. I'll talk with you about it Monday. Meanwhile we're having a party Saturday at our place. We'll expect you and Sarah."

Web wished he could refuse the invitation, but there was always business to consider; the Len Vember dealership billed far too much to incur displeasure, and unless he had a valid excuse,

Len would sense any reluctance to attend the party. A client could change agencies very easily. Accounts had been lost for even less than a refused invitation.

"We'll be there, Len," Web said, as heartily as he could. He supposed that for the chosen inner circle there would be the usual key game afterward. In the mood he was in now he would embrace the game. He was glad that Len did not hold it against him that Sarah didn't like the idea.

As a matter of fact, he was not certain that Len wasn't playing a long-term campaign to break down Sarah's defenses. Certainly there was more than friendliness in the looks that Len gave her; more than casual friendliness in the way he treated her; and an amused expression of secret knowledge in the way Maxine regarded Sarah, as if to say: *My husband wants to take you to bed, and is frustrated because you won't play with him.*

Vember seemed to be pleased with Web's acceptance of the invitation. They chatted a moment and hung up and Web left the agency.

A half-hour later he undressed in Aggie's bedroom. She had drawn the blinds and she was waiting for him with her eyes closed and her hands relaxed on either side of her pillowed head in a pose of surrender.

Moments later he bent over her and their kisses became hard and frantic in the mutual hunger of the two. Then they were together and it was as it always had been for them: uninhibited and self-centered as each took enjoyment from the other.

He was late getting home. Sarah had not bothered with dinner.

"I thought we'd eat out tonight," she said.

He nodded. He felt relaxed and satiated. His late afternoon hours with Aggie had been most satisfactory and he was glad that he had re-established the relationship. It was a good arrangement.

He needed a woman; especially a woman like Aggie. She didn't want marriage. She didn't want strings on him. She wanted from him exactly what he wanted from her, and the truth was recognized by both.

He looked more closely at Sarah, almost deliberately comparing his wife with the woman—his mistress, he supposed he should call her—he had just left.

The attentive scrutiny that he gave Sarah stirred a vague surprise and curiosity in him. There was a change in Sarah. She seemed to be softer, prettier, more relaxed. He thought he almost detected a blush on her cheeks, a glow that enhanced her features, and he realized—to his perplexity in the light of the preceding hours—that abruptly she was desirable as she had not been for months.

They ate at a neighborhood café and returned home. He turned on a TV set to check some commercials and then switched the set off and read. Sarah busied herself elsewhere in the house, and she had put records on the hi-fi phonograph.

It was not until they were preparing for bed that he remembered the Saturday night invitation from Len Vember. He mentioned it to Sarah.

"I think we'd better go," he said. "We can leave fairly early. They'll be playing their usual game afterward."

Sarah was in her bed adjusting a bedside reading lamp.

"A party might be fun," she said.

Web looked at her in surprise. "Oh? I thought you didn't like the Vember parties."

"There's too much drinking," she said. She opened a book and settled herself to read.

"And other things," he said cryptically. What kind of a game was she playing now? Why this suddenly affable voice and willingness to go to a party?

"You mean the key game?" she asked, without glancing at him. "They're still at it."

She shrugged a little and then gave him a look that was almost a taunt.

"Well, maybe it's interesting," she said.

He stared at her. "I don't believe you said that," he said. "Or are you doing the sauce-for-the-goose bit?"

"Why not?" she asked lightly.

Her unexpected attitude oddly disturbed him. Even in her coldness and strict conformity to conventions and to her concepts of morality, there had been a feeling of security that he had never quite acknowledged until this very moment. He had not necessarily liked it, and he had wanted a different set of standards for himself. But there had been a strange reliance upon the consistency of her attitudes; even if at times they served only as a target for his disapproval, scorn, ridicule and even anger.

He said skeptically, "Don't tell me you'd play the key game?"

She considered him silently for a half-minute, her mouth twisted in a quizzical smile.

"Yes, Web ... now I think I would—and *will*."

Her words disturbed him. His disdaining smile faded. "Why now?" he asked. "Why the big change?"

"I've decided to live differently," she said. She looked back at her book as if to end the conversation.

"How do you mean *differently?*" he asked.

"Good night, Web. I'm going to read—if it will disturb you I'll go into the guest room."

"One of us might as well be using the guest room," he snapped. "This is certainly not a marital bedroom. Not for months."

"Nor is it going to be. Not after that night six months ago—you and Agnes," she said evenly. "Never again. Do you want me to move into the guest room?"

Now she was smiling a deliberate taunt at him. His anger broke. He left his bed and leaned over her. He pulled down a shoulder strap of her nightgown and his hand reached for her.

"Damn you. You're my wife! Do you hear me? *My wife!* You can't talk to me this way! You can't treat me this way!"

"Take your hands off me."

"I'm going to—"

"No, Web. I mean it. Nothing. Neither by my granting you your so-called 'rights' nor by your trying to rape me. Is that clear?"

"What do you expect of me? Goddamn it! What do you expect me to do?" He was breathing hard in his anger and frustration and in a suddenly awakened desire that he could not too clearly understand.

"Do?" she smiled. "What you've always done. Go to Aggie. Go to your whore."

"Jesus! A man could kill you! You and your tongue and—"

She pulled his hands away from her and got out of bed and slipped into a robe. Carefully she turned out her individual bed lamp and picked up her book.

"I'm going to the guest room," she said calmly. "You don't excite me, frighten me or even impress me. Good night."

At the door she turned. "Be certain to tell Len Vember that I'll be happy to play their bedroom game after the party," she said. "Tell him that your wife is going to cut a small swath for herself."

"What in hell is wrong with you?" he shouted. "Talking like a—a—"

"A whore?" She laughed. "Why not? As you said—sauce for the goose."

She left the room. He heard the door to the guest room open and close. He heard the door lock snap into place.

Angrily he lit a cigarette and stared at the empty bed next to him. For a moment he was tempted to pick up the bedside telephone and dial Aggie's number, but he decided against it. Instead he got up and went downstairs to the kitchen. He got a bottle of bourbon out of a liquor cabinet and poured a large drink and gulped it down.

It was not until the warmth of the heavy drink had become effective that he could go to sleep.

CHAPTER THREE

T he West still is regarded as "new" country by many Easterners. Actually the newness is wearing off. The California '49-ers made their small stake in history well over a hundred years ago. Large portions of the West were settled immediately following the Civil War. A good many Western towns and cities have held their centennial celebrations, and segments of some of these cities already have been torn down for new building.

Len Vember was conscious of these truths. He also was very conscious of the business climate in the city where he lived. A great many of his fellow members of the Chamber of Commerce, the various other service clubs, the country club, and even the local automobile dealers' association were second and third generation residents. Not a few of them boasted of grandparents and great-grandparents who had come to this country in covered wagons.

Also there was a certain level of academic background (Ivy League, or Stanford, the other older West Coast colleges and universities, and a smattering of Midwestern schools were all represented) that was obvious in the rosters of presidents, vice-presidents and board members of the larger and better-established firms in the community. There was, as a matter of fact, a provincialism about the city that Len Vember and his wife well recognized and even respected—to a degree.

Among these native-born or well-established citizens of the city, Len Vember was a man apart; somewhat a man of mystery;

somewhat an enigma; and certainly a powerful figure of a man who had come to a community with next to nothing in his pockets and in a little over ten years had carved for himself a business of stature—at least in terms of sales volume and company earnings.

Carefully he had cultivated a casual and knowing smile when educational backgrounds were mentioned. Deliberately he had fabricated an acceptable biographical background for occasions when it might be demanded, speaking of his academic education by simply saying, "College—New York."

He had no living blood relatives, according to his story. He intimated, but never actually stated, that his was an old Eastern seaboard family.

After Len Vember began to make his mark in the community, his outstanding business success was all that was necessary to admit him to the places where he and his wife, Maxine, wanted to go. Both could be extremely gracious, on occasion. Both were good-looking. Len's gray hair (prematurely so since his twenties) gave him almost a handsome quality, especially when teamed with his flashing dark eyes and a deep tan that he maintained faithfully with golf in the summer and a sunlamp in the winter.

He had a good, solid, strong, male body. His features were equally good and strong. His voice was masculine, deep and rich. People liked him and he was a superb salesman.

Oddly, Maxine Vember was as vague about her background as her husband. She was rather tall, dark and of indeterminate age. She looked as if she might be in her mid-twenties, except that the knowing expression about her eyes and things she said might place her near her forties.

Actually she was in her mid-thirties, fifteen years younger than her husband. Her eyes were as dark as his. Her body was slim, contoured and full-breasted. Men usually looked at her twice. She could be a charming hostess. Women did not particularly like her, and they were afraid of her for some uneasy reason that few of them understood, except, perhaps, when they saw the way their husbands looked at her.

All in all, the Vembers had made their mark. They were established, accepted, invited and sought. Their entertaining was regarded as an ultimate in the city, and they had achieved such stature that certain post-party activities were kept a well-guarded secret, and the whole thing was considered to be smart because most of the strata of society involved—directly or indirectly—hated, above all, the thought that they might be "provincial."

The Vembers were "sophisticates"—they were above the usual cut—they had "something" that the native residents had missed somewhere along the line. They also had a large and expensive home, for Len Vember had built his meager beginnings into a very substantial bank account.

Two persons in the city actually knew the full story of the Vembers: Len and Maxine Vember. And they seldom spoke about the past. They were too content to accept the present and the future at face values. The past, in places, was too unpleasant to remember very often.

One of the few times that they deliberately remembered was one evening when they had dined at the home of a bank president. Len Vember had been made a member of the board of directors, and the dinner had been a pleasant, sedate affair that—to an extent—marked a small apex in the success story of Len Vember.

The dinner was over and they were home having a last drink before retiring. Maxine Vember approached mature beauty in the expensive and beautifully designed gown she wore. Len still wore a dinner jacket and might have just stepped off the set of a

Broadway production portraying the more exclusive and wealthy side of the American Way of Life.

Maxine was recalling her conversation with the bank president's wife.

"Her father started the bank," she told Len. "You probably know that. And her husband's father was on the board. This is all very blue chip, isn't it!" She smiled at her husband and took a sip of her drink. "Her biggest worry is that her daughter wants to go to some small Western school instead of Vassar."

"Problems," Len smiled. "What else?"

"It was all very social and gracious," Maxine said. "She did want to know where. we met."

"And you told her the usual?"

"Of course. Vaguely 'in Boston' and a quick change of subject." Maxine finished her drink and put down the glass. She looked again at her husband and apparently liked what she saw. "You're terrific in a dinner jacket, Len. I was watching you tonight. While she was asking me about us, I was thinking what would happen if I told her the truth."

"*That* would be terrific," Len smiled.

"Wouldn't it? Can't you hear me making with the truth? Like this: 'Where did we meet? Why, we met in a Detroit hotel room. I turned a twenty-dollar trick with him and he liked me so well he propositioned me to get out of the life.' "

"Christ!" Len Vember said and shook his head. "Don't even think about it, baby. Just look what we've got." He laughed. "Someone there remarked about the name—Vember. What nationality I am. I was indefinite—the lost in antiquity bit."

"Actually, how was it?" she asked feigning interest. She knew, but Len liked to tell the story to her. It was a sort of small summing up that he seemed to enjoy.

"I don't know who my father was," he said, the smile fading a little and his eyes going beyond her into meditation. "My mother died when I was a kid. She told me once that he was from Greece or Italy or somewhere down there. She wasn't very good with her geography. Nor her morals. Anyhow, she was using the name Agropillo. I didn't like it. It didn't mean anything to me. Joe Agropillo they called me. I didn't like the Joe, either.

"Then one night I was picked up in a rumble in the streets. I was still in my teens. The cops wanted a name when they got me to the station. On the spur of the moment I decided I was through with Joe Agropillo—spelling it out—saying I didn't know if it was Greek or what. A calendar was on the wall. It was early November. I figured they'd think 'November' would be a screwball name, so I simply took the 'Vember' part. I took 'Len'—I don't know why. Later I like the full name so well—when I got hep to changing names and had some money—that I had it made permanent in court."

"Some men wouldn't bother to make it legal," she said.

"I wanted it that way. I wanted to change everything about me to make it stick. Before I went into the army. And in school. That one year at City College. So I came up as Len Vember."

"Len Vember," she said thoughtfully. "I remember that first night. Did I ever tell you how scared I was that night?"

"You didn't act it."

"I was. A green kid from the wrong part of Dearborn. A kid with a Polish name no one could pronounce who had turned a few tricks by then. And when they said there was a call from some dealers who were in town, I didn't know what to expect. I thought maybe it would be Dearborn Inn—and I couldn't believe anything like that could ever happen there. I knew some of the help and they'd recognize me. I was relieved to learn it was in Detroit. But I still didn't know what was expected of me. Really."

"You did all right," he grinned.

She smiled thoughtfully and then her expression changed and she laughed a little.

"Did you know that Web Emmlin is from Ypsilanti?" she asked. "I've never told him I'm from Dearborn—only a few miles away."

"Don't. It's a good story working for us now. That Boston stuff. Let's leave it alone. Emmlin's a jerk."

Maxine eyed him with a knowing look. "But you don't feel that way about his wife," she said.

He shrugged and finished his drink. "You know how I am, baby."

"I know how you are, Len. And you know how I am. What do you suppose a head shrinker would say about us?"

"*Psychiatrist*, baby. Remember we're in the bankers' league this year. I suppose one would have a hell of a time with us."

"And to tell the truth, I don't think we're much different from any of the others. I notice that all of these upright young husbands enjoy me in the hay just as much as any other men once they've got around to it. How about the women?"

"We've talked about it before," he reminded her with a touch of amusement. He could almost see the excitement build in her eyes as she thought about it. Some psychiatrists maintained that the true nymphomaniac was a rare find, indeed. But this woman, his wife, was as close to being one as most men would ever find. As for himself ...

"They seem to like it, he nodded. "And so do I."

She crossed the room and leaned over and kissed him lightly. "You simply like sex, Len. Any way it comes. And you're good at it. Shall we have some?"

He laughed and pulled her down into his lap and kissed her hard. They looked into one another's eyes.

He said, "We've come a long way since that night in Detroit."

"You have, Len," she said, suddenly serious. "Have I kept up with you? I mean—well, sometimes I feel as if I'm out of my league. Like tonight. I'm just a kid from the wrong side of the tracks."

"You have it wrong, baby," he told her. "Not one of those dames is in your league."

The meaning of his words was completely understood between them. Actually there was a complete understanding between the two about most things. He was not surprised that she had detected his interest in Sarah Emmlin. She was right in suspecting that he would like to explore the relationships between a man and a woman that he might experience with Sarah Emmlin.

"Let's go to bed," he said. "It's a good idea."

For a long time he was to play a careful, waiting game for Sarah Emmlin. She had turned a cold shoulder to the key game, nor had he attempted to force the issue. He knew that Web Emmlin would have entered into the game without much urging, but for Sarah Emmlin to participate would mean a breakdown of self-imposed moral standards that were a far cry from the moral standards observed by the select post-party group.

Sooner or later, he told himself, there would be a change. Web could not hold a woman like Sarah Emmlin indefinitely. In time Web would get himself in a jam with another woman. When that happened, and when Sarah found out about it, she would be as likely to revolt against the security that had proved to be false as she would be likely to seek refuge from all men in a shell of bitterness.

Meanwhile, there were plenty of women to amuse him, and always there was his own wife, Maxine, who still could be the most exciting woman he ever had known. Her affairs and experiences with other men seemed only to whet his appetite for her, as he was certain his experiences with other women made him more exciting in her eyes.

Sometimes he wondered if it was not his appetite for women and sexual things that actually accounted for his financial success. Certainly he long ago had decided that money was the key to obtaining the excesses and variations that he wanted. When a man had enough money, he could buy what he wanted. When he had enough money, he could escape the restrictions—and usually the recriminations—that the less wealthy endured. And in his eyes, such restrictions and recriminations were to be endured—never accepted as being "normal" and never deserved.

Fully to understand Len and Maxine Vember, the objective observer probably would have to recognize that basically they both were amoral rather than immoral, and neither could remember when it really had been any different.

Certain important highlights stood out in Len's memory. His youth he tried to submerge; the poverty, the mother he never had actually loved, the scramble to stay alive and to follow out a grim determination to complete high school and get at least a taste of college.

Sometimes he wished he had known his father, and instinctively he felt that he had inherited a flair for bartering and acquiring wealth through some strain of blood that went back into the early days of Greece or Italy or one of the ancient countries. He also wondered if some of his appetites might not be as much a part of his ancestry as his knack for barter.

Certainly he had enjoyed his first girl as much as he had enjoyed driving through his first hard deal. They were two of the highlights.

The first business deal came through acquisition of a battered used car when he was hardly in his teens. He bought the battered jalopy for $37.50. He invested another $15 in it: a cheap paint job that he did himself, sawdust in a battered transmission, heavy oil, a set-back speedometer, lies and promises. He sold the car for $125. He was fifteen years old when he made the deal. The $37.50 he paid for the car came from the pocketbook of a drunk he had rolled one night.

He disliked rolling the drunk. He was smart enough to realize, even then, that it was smarter to take the suckers "within the law" rather than to risk a brush with the police. But he needed capital to get started.

He remembered his first girl just as vividly as he remembered the details of his first business deal.

She had come some time before the car deal. He had matured quickly and he had learned essential facts of life when he was young.

The girl lived in a flat in the same run-down building where Len and his mother lived. Her mother worked nights. Her father spent most of his time in taverns. She was as young as Len, and she, too, was maturing quickly.

Len made up his mind to have her, and he planned it carefully. He stole a half-pint of gin from the bottle his mother kept hidden in a closet. He bought a can of orange juice. Somewhere he had heard of the combination and the results that might be obtained.

He selected the place—the flat where he lived, and a night when his mother was working on one of the building cleaning jobs she sometimes held.

The girl drank the orange juice mixed half and half with gin. Len (he still was called Joe then) drank straight orange juice. He wanted nothing to dull the pleasure he anticipated.

By the time the girl had finished the half-pint of gin she was an easy conquest. She was a virgin and had admitted it to him during the preliminary love-making and fumbling. He shrewdly had anticipated what might happen—from what other boys had told him—and he found an old towel and doubled it under them. The bloodstains were absorbed by the towel and his bed was left clean.

The girl cried out in pain and then, surprisingly, she responded passionately and Len enjoyed her completely. The moment of conquest was one of intense pleasure and physical delight for him.

He felt a surge of thanksgiving that it was possible to enjoy a woman in this manner, and he had been almost gentle in the taking, as if already he had become the connoisseur—the libertine—who knew the greater delights and satisfactions of the leisurely feast. Certainly the enjoyment of a woman was almost an accomplished art for him from the first time.

Many years later a strange thing was to come from this first possession of a woman. The girl had become a woman and a wife and mother. Occasionally she met Len on the street and sometimes they had coffee together. Nothing else was between them except this friendliness from their youth and the fact that they once had known one another intimately.

On one of these days, years later, they talked about it frankly and she smiled as she put down a coffee cup and looked across a small table in a crowded, busy coffee shop where they had met by accident.

"Joe—I mean, *Len*—you know I'm happily married and have fine kids and a good husband. I wouldn't cheat for anything in the world. Even with you!" She laughed a little. Then she blushed slightly and said, "But I always wanted to thank you for—well, that first time. You did it so nicely—so gently, I guess. I've always been thankful for that. It—it helped me become a woman so easily ... and so well."

Len sometimes thought of this as one of the finest compliments he ever had received. Making love, from that beginning, was an art for him—a goal in itself ... a skill to be acquired and perfected. Sex was of paramount importance to him. Business and sex. Business and women. Money and women. And, of course, the money could buy the women. Meanwhile, he sometimes acquired a similar satisfaction in consummating a sharp business deal that he did in conquering a new woman.

It was typical of him that he had used some of his profit from the sale of the used car to buy another battered car for resale. He had put some of the proceeds in a bank for working capital, and he had bought his first hour with a prostitute to experience one or two mild deviations that he had heard about.

Following the war Len went into a car dealership. Within a year he was sales manager. Within two years he was part owner of the dealership. He sold out in the third year and parlayed a modest financial backlog with his reputation for selling cars into his own dealership in the Western city that appealed to him. The factory was willing to back him to a degree. He applied "hard sell" practices and concentrated on "volume selling." He went into financing, realizing that he frequently could make more profit from finance charges than from the sales profit of the cars he sold. Within ten years he was comparatively well-to-do and solidly entrenched in the city.

So much for his business life. His sexual life—which was so vitally important to him—also progressed.

His relationship with Maxine truly had begun when she was a call girl. She pleased him enough that he wanted to keep her. She understood him well enough to know that he would always want other women. She didn't mind—because she wanted other men.

With the passing years, Len's appetite swerved away from the women he could acquire for money to the women who were not so easy to obtain. He began to notice and desire other men's wives. He sought new excitements to whet an appetite that could become jaded by the easily obtained. He began to realize that possibly the excitement of the chase could be even more exciting than enjoyment of the victim after she was caught. But even with the dull victims there could be excitement.

A woman—the wife of one of his salesmen who later left the city with his family—wisely explained some of Len to himself.

Her seduction had been slow. It had taken well over a year. It had been accomplished only after many drinks one night when he had sent the husband back East to a factory meeting and the wife had gone for a ride with Len when he suggested that he wanted to talk with her about her husband's future.

Possibly she had anticipated Len's intentions—she was a discerning woman, he later realized—and thought she could handle any situation. And, quite probably, she had believed her husband's job to be in jeopardy. At any rate, she had gone with him. They had dined at a roadside place that was noted for an expensive atmosphere and strong drinks.

The night had progressed to more drinks then she should have taken, a night ride, and a stop at Len's summer place in the mountains "just to show you what it's like."

There had been a couple of additional drinks, double for her, the potency concealed by mix. Perhaps her inhibitions had fallen away, or perhaps she simply had not known what Len was doing with her.

Whatever the reason, when she had awakened some time later in a bed at the summer place, she was fairly sober and fully aware that Len had enjoyed her. Nor had she resisted when he had taken her again. Possibly her failure to resist was because

Len had displayed a surprising skill in love-making. Never had she experienced physical sensations such as he had aroused. Compared with Len, her husband's love-making was like a boy's.

Weeks later, in the same cabin, but in the afternoon, she participated in love-making that she hardly believed possible a few weeks before—things she had only read or vaguely heard about.

Afterward she lay exhausted, half-smiling as she looked up at him.

"You don't seduce women," she told him quietly. "You debauch them. You corrupt them. You teach them to enjoy and want and finally to need things that other men may be unwilling to give them. You've corrupted me."

"And you like it?" he smiled, and bent his head to the warm flesh of her body. "Like this?"

"Oh, yes," she whispered and then she gasped. "Oh, God, yes ... yes!"

Len always remembered what she had said and acknowledged to himself that he had deliberately set out upon a voyage of corruption in the city. The "key game" had been his *coup d'état*. With it he had managed to corrupt couple after couple, wives and husbands, and to obtain for his own use an exciting menu of women, even as Maxine had been able to indulge her demands for variety.

Money had been important to accomplishing all this. Money had enabled him to build the house, the pool, the party room with the movie projector that he used to run "stag films."

The stag films had been one of the opening wedges. First he had shown them to some of the men. Maxine had shown them to a few selected wives. Gradually they had run the films for husbands and wives together.

Eventually he and Maxine had introduced the late night swimming parties "in the nude." Always there was plenty to drink. Always the films were shown. Always there were convenient guest rooms with doors that could be locked.

By the time he was ready to suggest the "key game" he already had enjoyed a good many of the women, and Maxine had managed to assuage her desires with most of the husbands involved. The key game was a natural step of progression in the corruption that Len Vember had planned.

Occasionally a couple dropped out of the "inner circle" for one reason or another, and occasionally a new couple was admitted after what Len secretly called the "softening up before the hard sell."

"It's not too unlike selling cars," he once told Maxine. "You built up the desire to the point where the customer will pay anything—agree to almost any terms—to get what he, or she, wants. Most selling is based on emotions, anyhow.

"Of course, people buy for security, shelter, food—the necessities. But they also buy for status, to impress, to enjoy luxury, to feel important. Some people try to be sensible and not fall for the hard sell, but salesmen and advertising people have learned all the weak spots.

"It gets to the point where a man will mortgage a big slice of his pay checks for thirty months or more to buy a car that within twelve months isn't worth the balance he still owes. He'll cry to high heaven if he thinks a bank wants to charge six per cent on a straight loan, but he'll pay eighteen per cent financing a car that he wants."

"And mortgage his soul and marriage for a good roll in the hay with someone besides his wife," Maxine smiled.

"You're so right, baby!"

On the day that Len Vember asked Web and Sarah Emmlin to the Saturday night party, he believed there was a possibility that Sarah Emmlin might finally participate in the key game.

As a matter of fact, he was suspicious that she and Carl Trojan might already be playing games in Carl Trojan's cabin out in the hills. That would be the place to which Trojan probably would take her, and Len had almost an occult ability to sense when an affair was taking place.

He had seen the glances that passed between Sarah and Carl; the casual touching of hands and bodies; the contemplative expression in Carl's eyes when he looked at Sarah Emmlin when she had her back turned to him. Len knew that expression in a man's eyes—the contemplation of viewing what he was going to have.

In a way Len was sorry that Carl Trojan might get to her before he, Len, probably could. But he was practical enough to appreciate that the breaking down of barriers by Carl Trojan would make it easier later on for Len Vember. And Len was certain that Trojan could not teach her as much as he could teach her. Carl Trojan might seduce her into adultery, but Len Vember could corrupt her into debauchery.

Meanwhile, another bit of business was ready for his attention.

After talking with Web Emmlin, he flipped a key on an intercommunication box. His secretary in an outer office—he disdained the use of the glassed-in office some dealers preferred—answered his call.

"I'm expecting Mr. Alexis and some others with him," he said.

"They're waiting," she told him.

"I'll see them."

In a moment she ushered in four men. Alexis was dark-complexioned, fairly young, energetic-appearing. The others belonged to the same team. Two carried brief cases. A third carried a large, leather portfolio and a folding tripod. While he set up the tripod, one of the others took mounted charts and artwork from the leather portfolio. Meanwhile, Alexis was busy shaking hands with Vember and introducing his companions.

"This group," Alexis assured Vember, "comprises probably the most powerful advertising team in this area."

Alexis questioned his cohorts with raised eyebrows. They nodded that they were ready to go to work. He looked again at Vember.

"Is there anyone else you'd like to have in for the presentation?" he asked. "Your sales manager, perhaps?"

Len shook his head. "I own the business," he smiled. "I hire the help, call the turns, pay the bills, and I select the ad agency I want."

"Certainly. We prefer it that way," Alexis agreed. "We'd rather deal with just one person in a firm."

"All right. Let's see what you have to offer."

Alexis efficiently launched into the presentation. The team was well co-ordinated. The advertising was sharp. The proposed campaigns appeared to have merit.

Len listened and watched with an impassive expression. His was not a big account in terms of Madison Avenue bigness, but it was large in relation to other accounts on the local scene.

"Two things always have been apparent to us," Alexis pointed out. "First, you are the largest volume dealer in the area. Second, you believe in spending money on advertising to obtain volume and subsequent profit from that volume. Our intent is to increase the impact of your advertising to a full realization of the sales potential you have within your grasp. We know that we can do the job for you."

Len thought how many times he had heard Web Emmlin say virtually the same thing. Did they think that they were telling him something that he didn't know? Hell! He'd taught *them!* But he needed creative people to write and produce the hard selling spots and ads. He needed an agency to handle the details of buying time and space and taking care of the trivia.

Actually, an agency didn't cost him much. The media usually paid most of the bill—and the full cost of advertising was passed on to the customers, anyhow. So he really was shopping for good sales talent. And in this area Alexis and his crew of eager young men might have something. Web was dragging a little, despite the fair results from the last spots.

"We believe that you need much more significant TV," Alexis said, beginning his summary. "We'd like to do more radio saturation with production spots. We'd like to place greater emphasis upon your corporate image, as it were, and to keep you supplied with a constantly varied, exciting procession of campaigns that really will be effective. We have the agency—the people—to do the job for you."

He continued his summary, pacing it carefully, and making certain not to overdo it. He realized as well as Len did that Web Emmlin was in the background; that this was deliberate poaching on a competitor's territory; but Alexis was young, ruthless and smart.

"And that's the ball of wax, Mr. Vember," he concluded.

The rest of the Alexis team began to gather their presentation materials and to pack them. Alexis frankly contemplated Len's face, searching for an expression that might indicate the prospect's reaction to the presentation.

Len smiled. "It was a good job. There are other factors to consider. Don't push me. I'll let you know within two weeks."

"Fair enough," Alexis said. "We're confident that we can do the job you want done. Let us know—and I sincerely hope that we'll be working together very soon."

Len accompanied them to the door and watched them leave. An attractive young woman sat in the outer office, obviously waiting for him. Len glanced at his secretary. "Hold my calls," he said. He looked at the young woman. "Mrs. Lancotte ... you want to see me?"

"Yes." She stood and came toward him. He stepped back and followed her into his office. She walked across the room and took the chair that Alexis had been using. Len went around his desk and sat down. He smiled at the young woman, enjoying the contrast of dark brown eyes and golden hair, the smooth and youthful curves of her body beneath a simple sheath summer dress.

"Well?" he said.

"Mr. Vember, I simply can't raise the money. I've already been to your finance office and Mr. Waltwyler said I'd have to see you again."

"When we talked last week you seemed certain you could raise the money at once," Len said. "It was only because we felt that your husband, in his position with the investment company, was a good credit risk that we allowed you to get two payments behind. Three is more serious for us—"

"He doesn't make a big salary, Mr. Vember. You must realize that he's just beginning with the company. That's why we need such a long-term contract on the car and—"

"I understand that. But you're three months behind in payments now. You owe us almost two hundred and fifty dollars. I'm afraid I'll have to ask you for the keys to the car."

"You can't—!"

"As a matter of fact, Mr. Waltwyler called your husband last week. Your husband said there must be some mistake. That you told him you'd sent in the payments on time every month. I told Mr. Waltwyler not to press it until we saw you again. We wouldn't want any trouble between you and your husband, Mrs. Lancotte."

"I appreciate that—I mean, not pressing Harold. He asked me if I'd sent in the payments. I lied. I said I had—that there must be a mistake and that'd straighten it out. I thought I could raise the money."

"Did you raise it?"

"No."

"How did you try to get it? Borrow it?"

She looked down at her lap, her fingers nervously opening and closing her handbag.

"I haven't any place to borrow money," she said. "I managed to raise a little—I pawned a portable typewriter."

"Not enough to help much," Len smiled.

"Of course not." She looked up at him. "I used it to play the horses. I lost. That's where the car payments went, too. If Harold knew, he'd—well, I don't know *what* he'd do. I just don't dare tell him. He hates gambling and everything that goes with it. He's so straight-laced about everything. Especially since he's been on this job. They wouldn't like it if they knew that his wife—well, you can see what I mean...."

"You're in a spot," Len nodded.

"I'm in a terrible spot," she said. "I can tell you one thing—if I ever get out of this one I'll never look at a horse again."

"I can understand that. But meanwhile, we have a business to run. I'm sorry. I'm afraid I'll have to ask for the keys to the car. We'll have to repossess."

She stared at him and the tip of her tongue wet her lips. Her eyes betrayed her worry and fright.

"Isn't there some way?" she asked. "I'd do—*anything.*"

"That's a big promise," Len smiled.

"I'm afraid of what Harold will do. Frankly, it's happened before. Losing money I was supposed to use for other things. The last time he said we would be finished if he ever learned that I was gambling again."

"I'm sorry."

"Can't you—? I mean, whatever you say, Mr. Vember. Even for a little more time. I could pay it all back in three months. I can get a job. Maybe I can pay it back in two months. Just as long as Harold never knows …"

Len didn't speak. He sat quietly and looked at her, his eyes upon her hair, her features, her smooth throat, and the full curve of her breasts above the slim waist and tapering thighs.

"Bluffing?" he said.

"No." She stared at him defiantly.

He stood and went to the door. He flipped over the door bolt and turned to look at her. She had been watching him.

"Three months," he said.

"Three months."

"All right," he nodded. "Let's see now if you're bluffing."

Slowly she stood. She looked around the room. There was no window. An air conditioner hummed quietly. She glanced at the locked door. She looked across the room at the large couch by the far wall. She looked back at Len.

She said, "I'm glad you're a good-looking man. I hate what I'm about to do—but maybe it'll be a pleasure … with you."

"I didn't think you'd be so frank."

"I can be. Any woman can be when she has to bargain with what makes her a female. A woman can be a real bitch, Mr. Vember."

"You surprise me a little."

"I surprise myself sometimes. I'm not a cheap pick-up, Mr. Vember. I'm a fairly nice, clean university graduate married to a man she met in school. And I'm a compulsive gambler. That's my flaw. This time I was caught. I always have believed that you should pay up when you're caught—especially when it's your own damned fault. Can I ask one thing?"

"Certainly."

She reached behind her and unfastened a snap at the top of the sheath and zipped open the dress.

"Please use some protection," she said. "I don't want to get more than I'm bargaining for."

Len laughed in his quick enjoyment of this frank and practical woman. She promised more than he had expected.

"I took care of that five years ago," he said. "A vasectomy."

She nodded knowingly and reached down for the hem of her dress to whisk the material over her head. She wore no hose, and only panties and a brassiere under the dress.

"All right," she said. "I'm ready to pay up—whenever you're ready to collect."

An hour later, a few moments after she had dressed and left Vember's office, Jenny Lancotte stopped in a telephone booth and dialed a number. A man's voice answered.

"I'm on my way home, honey," she said. "Or do you want to meet me downtown for dinner?"

"I'll meet you at Mac's Place," the man said. "But how did it go?"

"Harold, honey—he bought it! We've got it made. Wait until you hear!"

CHAPTER FOUR

Maxine Vember turned the volume of the hi-fi phonograph so low that the Mancini music from *Mr. Lucky* would be only a pleasant background for the telephone call she was about to make.

She dialed a number and a soft feminine voice answered. Maxine pictured the woman at the other end of the line; visualized the soft brown hair that framed the very feminine and pretty features, the brown eyes, the full lips, the delicately molded body. Altha Gateson was in her late twenties, married to Tom Gateson, who was a few years older.

Tom Gateson's rise in a utility company had been rapid and expected because his father was one of the most important stockholders and president of the board. However, young Gateson had not attained his vice-presidency so quickly solely because of his father. He had ability, drive and other attributes that would have assured him a fair chance of quick advancement anywhere. His educational background was thorough and carefully planned. His body was fit and trim as becomes a man who has had the finest medical attention, grooming and care.

His marriage to Altha had been a social event in the city. She came from a pioneer family. To all appearances this should be a successful marriage. In some aspects it was. In some it was not.

Again there were hidden undercurrents, concealed facts, undetected incidences, and the personal histories that shape lives.

For one thing, Tom Gateson's apparent industry and family-insured respectability concealed his tendency to indulge occasionally in unconventional happenings. In college he had been in trouble several times, mostly in episodes involving drinking and girls.

Later, after his marriage, he found a measure of satisfaction and release in his job. But not enough release to prevent him from playing hard when he played, because he did most things intensely. Strange and uneasy forces frequently drove him into excesses.

The accepted respectability and society-page event of Tom's and Altha's marriage hinted at the traditional love affair that welded together two of the city's oldest and wealthiest families; a marriage flavored by Junior League excitement; a bachelor dinner at the University Club; and all the traditional elements that made one of the "outstanding social events of the season."

Virtually no one other than the bride and bridegroom knew that the bride was almost four months pregnant at the time of the wedding. When the couple returned from their honeymoon, Tom suggested a local abortionist again.

Altha had resisted the suggestion before the marriage, largely through fear of discovery and because Tom could not bring enough pressure to make her go through with it.

After the wedding, she dreaded the certain stigma of a "five-months baby" even more than she realized she would, and Tom's urging became more powerful. Tom did not want children "yet." He wanted to get "set."

She had the abortion as soon as she could after the honeymoon. Since then, at Tom's behest, she had taken careful precaution to avoid encountering the same trouble again, for Tom was quite outspoken in his opinions about not wanting children. As a matter of fact, Altha lately was not certain that he wanted a wife. Things were very unsettled behind the door of the split-level house in the suburban hills where they recently had settled.

For the last six months, before this afternoon's call from Maxine, the Gatesons had become part of the larger group that partied regularly with the Vembers. Furthermore, they knew about the inner circle and its activities, and had been invited to participate. Until now they had not, but there were ample indications that the idea was acceptable to Tom Gateson, and Maxine Vember had carefully nourished his interest.

Maxine was very much aware of these things when she heard Altha answer the telephone, and she also suspected that Altha was worried. If Tom Gateson had problems arising from his driving energy, desires and demands, Altha, too, had problems.

Altha's largest problem was simply that she was in love with her husband. If she pretended to enjoy the Vember early evening parties, it was because she was afraid of Tom's displeasure if she suggested that she did not. If she noticed his increasing interest in Maxine Vember, she tried to protect herself in a cloak of casual acceptance of her husband's "flirtation."

Deep inside, Altha was frightened. Maxine knew it so well that she was certain that Altha was ready to do almost anything to keep her husband, even if it meant drastic means to prevent his displeasure, or to make him feel that she was equal to his drives, or that she still was desirable in the eyes of other men. Maxine appreciated the many "motivational urges" (as Len liked to call them) that might conceivably prompt a woman to act against her nature.

It was time to lay the groundwork toward completion of her own plans. Tom Gateson was ready and now the rest was up to her.

"Altha," she said sweetly, "we're having a party Saturday night. Of course we'll expect you and Tom. Len's probably told Tom about it, but I wanted to check it out with you."

"We'll be happy to come," Altha said, her voice somehow failing to match the enthusiasm of the words themselves. "We haven't a thing planned and I'm certain that Tom will be delighted."

"A few are staying on afterward," Maxine said. "We'd like to have you."

"Oh, Maxine ... I don't know!"

She's frightened, Maxine thought. "Well, don't worry about it now, dear," she said. "We'll talk about it then. I just thought I'd let you know that we'd love to have you two with us."

"I—I *do* appreciate it," Altha faltered. "It's just ... well, I'll talk with Tom."

"Of course. Len may mention it to him, too. And Altha ..." Maxine hesitated and allowed a small giggle to filter over the wire, doing it lightly and well." Just in case—maybe you'd better be prepared before you leave home. You never know what will happen and you and Tom may decide to try it just once."

"Oh ...?" Altha's voice was uncertain. Then she said, "Oh, I see."

Maxine laughed, spoke a few more words and a few moments later the two women hung up.

Maxine thoughtfully returned to the record player and turned up the volume. She remembered her conversation with Tom Gateson earlier in the week, his questions about the key game, and his obvious interest.

"Can you rig the game?" he had asked.

She had shrugged. "There's a way."

"I'd like that. I mean, if I could rig it with you."

"Would you?" she had asked with a sly smile.

"Try me."

So you want to play games, she had thought as she looked at him. *Maybe you think you can teach me things, but I'll teach you, big boy! I'll teach you things you never dreamed existed. So you'll never want that sweet, pretty wife of yours again. Or maybe you can teach her then. She could learn a lot. I'm certain of that. I can understand why a man would want to teach her things. She's really lovely—just inexperienced.*

The Mancini music ended and she flipped the record and started the other side. She smiled as she recalled her brief conversation with Altha. It was part of the softening process, the "pre-selling" that Len talked about, and she knew that Len already had talked with Tom and had received assurance that the couples probably would stay for games after the party. As yet—obviously from the conversation with Altha—Tom had not broached the idea to his wife, but he would.

"And she'll do it because she's afraid of him—or of losing him," Maxine told herself. "And I'll have Tom in her bed when he takes me home. Not his bed—hers! I'd like that!"

Deep restlessness began to stir in her and she wished it could happen now—here—anywhere. It was like a frantic disease—this constant, driving need for a man. She mustn't think about it yet. It was bad enough waiting without thinking about it.

After a moment she dialed the dealership. A secretary said that Len was in conference. She'd have him call.

"Just tell him we're eating early and to come straight home," Maxine said. They would not eat early because she would be waiting upstairs in the bedroom and Len would know how to take care of the hunger that really plagued her.

After Altha finished her conversation with Maxine she went out to the patio and a few more minutes of afternoon sun. She wore a halter and shorts. Her skin was beautifully tanned, and she had a firmed, smoothly curved, accented lushness of body that was extraordinarily female and sexual.

She stretched out on a sun cot. The afternoon was waning, but the sun still was hot enough to bathe her in lassitude and weakening, almost sensual warmth.

Maxine's suggestion had frightened her to the point where she wished she could block it completely from her mind. Only that wouldn't solve anything. From the first time she had learned about the key game she knew that eventually she would have to face the problem it presented. She knew that Tom would want to become a member of that inner group.

She was married to Tom, and once she had been pregnant by him—before that hour in the abortionist's office in an old building. She knew more than she wanted to know about Tom Gateson, her husband.

She knew, for instance, that sometimes he slept with other women in New York when he went there on business—and probably in other cities. He frankly had told her about the New York women in an outburst of sadistic ridicule during a high point in one of their quarrels.

"Don't talk to me about a husband's duty to his wife!" he had snapped at her in the altercation that had started from a trivial incident. "My duty to respect you? Honor you? Cherish you? What about your duties to me? My God, you're not even a good lay! I've had better from call girls in New York. A hell of a lot better. And if that shocks you, ask yourself why I'd be interested in a call girl for a night!"

"Damn you!" she had cried in frustrated shock and anger. "Why do you do these things to me? *Why?* I *married* you. I listened to you and—"

"Yes, you listened to me! You listened and acted as if you knew what it was all about and got yourself pregnant. I married you, all right. Because you were pregnant. Remember? You wouldn't talk abortion until after you'd hooked me. Then it was all right. Then you'd have the abortion!"

"How can you say that? We were in *love!* You know how it was. Before I got pregnant. After we found out." Tears had started to run down her cheeks and her voice reflected the anguish of deep hurt.

After a moment some of the anger had gone from his eyes.

"All right. I'm sorry I said that. Maybe it was love—or whatever you call it at that age. Love—hot pants—something. But you're right. It takes two to tango."

"But don't you feel anything for me now? Tom—there must be something ...?" She had been unable to disguise the sudden fright that crept into her voice.

"Skip it," he had said in a resigned tone. "Just skip it. We're married. Let it go at that."

"Tom—do you want a divorce?"

"I didn't say that. Maybe—maybe I want more freedom for a while. Maybe I have to find out what I want."

"But what about *me,* Tom? What happens to *me?* I love you. Can't you understand that? I *love* you."

"I understand it. I appreciate it, Altha. Let's just not confuse love and sex. That was *my* mistake."

She had stared at him through the distortion brought by tears in her eyes. She had said, "Oh, Tom—we're so mixed up—so terribly mixed up...."

He had left her and had gone out to return stumbling drunk early in the morning; to pull the bedclothes from her, to fumble for her body, and to fail miserably in his effort to possess her.

Altha still shuddered at the memory of that night, but it had been one of the times that had warned her that sooner or later she would have to suffer more if she stayed with Tom, and if she wanted to hold him.

Saturday night, she thought. Despite the heat of the sun, she felt a cold contraction of muscles as if to protect her vulnerability.

She never had known another man intimately. Tom had been the first and only man to have her. The thought of another man was difficult for her to conceive, even in fantasy.

Sometimes she forced herself to think about Tom and other women—of a call girl in New York. What did a girl like that do to make herself more satisfactory to Tom than the things she tried to do? What was wrong?

She had read the various marriage manuals she could obtain. She had tried to employ the suggestions they made. She often had pretended an ecstasy that she did not actually feel, yet she knew that she was not what the doctors described as "frigid." She almost always experienced a climax with Tom, but it was never a wild, overpowering experience for her. Not once had it ever been.

Usually it was a gradual building of sensation that finally overflowed into a gentle, pulsating sensation, that she was powerless to stop, and which had almost an anesthetic effect leaving her too weak to move or to react. It was a transient thing that was briefly pleasant and satisfying, but never an exciting, exuberant experience to throw her into chaotic movement, moaning or tears.

"*Do* something!" Tom sometimes demanded in frustration. "*Do* something!" And she obediently simulated the movements and excitement he seemed to expect, even while she experienced nothing to inspire them. She supposed that a call girl would be adept at this sort of thing.

As a matter of fact, she suspected that prostitutes usually pretended excitement. She had read something about that in one of the marriage manuals, or was it one of the Kinsey books?

The Kinsey books had revealed startling findings about the relationships between men and women. Adultery was much more common than she ever had suspected. The numbers and percentages had set her friends to talking, with more than one speculative observation and raising of eyebrows.

Possibly she was being much too conservative in a progressive world. Possibly she was wrong in adhering so strictly to her marriage vows. Certainly, before her marriage, she had failed to preserve her chastity. She could have been included in the startling high total of females who had experienced "premarital intercourse." She had engaged not only in premarital intercourse, but premarital pregnancy as well, she thought. And she could have been counted in the abortion reports subsequently released in another Kinsey report.

The sun brought small beads of perspiration to her forehead. She stretched luxuriously. "Maybe there's more to it than I know," she said to herself. "Maybe Tom doesn't truly awaken me. Only, it would have to come from a greater gentleness and understanding of my femininity—the things that please me. He doesn't know. He never has known!"

From the thought came another furtive prodding and she dared to think about the key game. If Tom had been with other women, why shouldn't she—at least just once—be with another man? Perhaps there were things to learn. If she could think of it as a call girl must think of it—just a physical relationship without depth or meaning other than physical, sensory reactions ... certainly a person could be intelligent and logical enough to accept it for what it essentially was—as a physical experience. Others did....

She slept and when she awoke Tom was home. He brought drinks out on the patio and seemed to be in a jovial mood.

"Len called," he said. "They want us for a party Saturday night."

"I know. Maxine called."

"Did she mention the bit of business after the main party?"

Altha felt the fear again, but she sipped her drink and looked over the rim of her glass at Tom. He was watching her with a glow of suppressed excitement in his eyes. He wanted to take part in those after-party games of adultery! He wanted her to take part. She could sense it in his expression, the look in his eyes, the excitement in his voice.

"She mentioned it," Altha said.

"Well?"

"Do you want us to do that?"

"What do *you* think?"

He wants me to say yes, she thought. *But he doesn't want to order me to do it. He's retaining that much decency. But he wants to, and if I don't he'll resent it. And if that's what he wants me to do, I'll do it. Maybe it will make a difference for us. Maybe there's some jealousy left. Something. God knows he's bruised my feelings for him until there isn't anything left but this numb, unreasonable love that he hasn't bruised quite enough to kill.*

"All right," she said. "Let's stay."

He looked surprised, but the excitement leaped higher in his eyes. "You mean it?" he asked.

"If you don't mind letting another man take me to bed."

He stood and went to the cot and sat beside her. His hands touched her.

"Maybe you'll like it," he smiled. "Maybe it'll be good for us. You're good in bed ..."

"You haven't said *that* very often," she said, conscious of his hands upon her, and suddenly catching the fever of excitement from him. "Maybe I'll be better after someone else. Is that what you think?"

He bent suddenly and kissed her. His hands became more demanding and the halter came loose.

"Not here," she whispered. "Not out here. Inside."

"Hurry."

He picked her up and carried her inside. Urgency was upon them and she shut her eyes and clutched at him. He lowered her to their bed and she heard the sounds of his undressing, felt the haste with which he stripped the shorts from her, and then his whispered question: "Is it safe?"

"Yes ... yes ... go ahead ..."

His hands cupped under her. The excitement was intense and turbulent and exhausting for him. At first she experienced some of it with him and then it subsided to passive reception and the slow, steady climb to the peak and the gentle easing over into gentle pulsation and controlled spasms of groin and body. It was over and gone as easily as that for her. It was violent for him.

Afterward she realized that she had forgotten to stimulate the reaction she knew he wanted from her.

He rolled free of her and after a moment he said, "That was good for me. But maybe an experience will make it better for you. You don't *do* anything ..."

PART II

THE GAME

CHAPTER FIVE

In Vembers' party room the only light was the illumination reflected from the silver movie screen. The air was heavy with cigarette smoke and the smell of many drinks. The only sounds came from the mechanical stutter of a movie projector and the breathing of the few couples in the room.

On the screen a young, nude woman and a nude man performed sexually. The motion picture was lewdly graphic and without a sound track.

The couples who watched already had paired off for their key game partnerships of the night. They sat or sprawled on sofas or floor cushions.

Len Vember, who was operating the projector, mused that the movie was not likely to greatly arouse most women; that only a few women might enjoy it. However, a woman might not be immune to the letdown of inhibitions that mixed-company viewing of the picture might cause.

Beside him Sarah watched the movie with mixed emotions, none of them particularly concerned with what she saw. The sexual athletics of the couple on the screen were of little interest to her. It was a vulgar display, a small boy chalking four-letter words on a sidewalk, salesmen telling off-color jokes in the men's room.

Of greater concern to her at the moment was the realization that she and Len Vember were mated for the night as a result of the key selection a short time before. Very soon the others would leave—Web and Altha, Tom with Maxine—and Len Vember would escort her to a room in this house where she would be expected to undress and share a bed with him.

She glanced at Len and saw that he was not watching the picture.

"Bore you?" he asked, nodding toward the screen.

"Yes."

"I thought so. It does most women—except some like Maxine. She admires techniques."

"You don't?"

"Certainly. But not on display, and those two on the screen are amateurs. They're stupid—stupid or they wouldn't allow themselves to be photographed like that."

"Maybe they're exhibitionists."

He shrugged. "I doubt it. They did it for money. Not kicks."

"Why do you show the pictures?"

"Usually it's a big deal for the men. And it has a certain demoralizing effect upon the women. Seems to make it easier for them to play games later on. The effect's more obvious when more couples are watching."

"You seem to know a lot about it, Len."

"I do."

"I'm afraid I can't live up to what you may expect," she said. She was trying to make talk now. Actually she wasn't quite certain that she wanted to go through with it. Committing adultery with Carl had been one thing—going to bed with Len Vember was something else. Only—and she recognized the thought—Len Vember had a way of letting a woman know that he was experienced and that he might be exciting.

"Nervous?" he asked.

"Perhaps," she admitted. "And cautious. I'm not certain."

"It doesn't have to be that personal," he smiled. "We don't have to become emotionally involved. I genuinely like you. I want to please you."

"You wouldn't feel that way about it if you didn't think I'd please you."

"I won't deny that."

"So we're back where we started. I'll probably disappoint you."

"You couldn't," he said. "You don't know my likes and dis-likes—or whether or not you would disappoint me. I'm the judge of that. And I know before we start. I'll show you what I mean later."

He glanced at the picture and added, "Please don't worry. There's nothing to worry about."

Nothing to worry about, she thought. *Nothing and everything.*

She remembered her afternoon with Carl and what had led to it. Carl was her first transgression into unfaithfulness, and she was reasonably certain that she was his first.

It was easy to be naïve about the relationships between men and women, and about the individuals themselves. There was no certainty that Carl had not been having affairs with a dozen different women, only she was reasonably positive that he had not.

Carl had the analytical, orderly, functional mind of the engineer. He was the builder. He lived in a world of facts and tangibles. Somehow it seemed incongruous to picture Carl men-tally—the engineer, mathematician, builder—as being greatly concerned with emotions, the subtleties of lovemaking, or the complexities of man-and-woman relationships.

Certainly Carl was not preoccupied with sex. As far as that was concerned, she wondered how many actually were. Len? Probably he was, judging by what was happening tonight. Sex was important to him, as it obviously was to his wife.

Sarah looked at her husband where he sat with Altha Gateson. *Web's immature,* she said to herself. *He's never quite grown up. He doesn't know what he really wants of a woman, and he isn't capable of giving too much. His sex drive excites him, but it doesn't drive him. He never did to me what Carl did.*

She wondered what it would be like between Web and Altha, and smiled a trifle. It wouldn't be good for them. Web was not strong—sexually nor in any other way. And Altha looked as nervous and uneasy as Web did. They were playing in a game that was over their heads, and Sarah knew it.

Aloud she said, "It separates the men from the boys, I guess."

Len looked at her quizically. "Secret thought?" he asked.

She smiled. "An expression my father used."

"Meaning?"

"It's too nebulous to explain. This picture is horrible. It's obscene."

Len nodded complacently. "It fascinates Web—and embarrasses him because you're here watching it, and because he's with Altha. He doesn't know what he should say or do."

"And Altha?"

"Disgusted. Shocked. She didn't think people could do the things she's watching. She's almost ready to panic, but she's not willing to admit that she's naïve. She's resigned to accepting this as sophistication—but she's scared to death and using vodka for courage."

"Tom?"

"Look at him. Excited. Maxine's hands are on him. She's teasing him."

On the screen the performers were engaged in their ugly pastime and despite Sarah's instinctive loathing of the picture, she found her eyes caught to the screen as if by a compelling magnet. She watched the convulsive movements of the girl on the screen and suddenly felt a startling, perverted pleasure in viewing the capture and possession of the other woman.

The girl's face became contorted with the sensuality of the moment as the man's efforts became vigorously rapacious.

Sarah breathed more rapidly, and she felt Len's hand firmly on her thigh. The room seemed to be charged with tenseness as her glance flashed from one face to another, and the varied expressions were imprinted on her mind.

Altha Gateson watched the screen with the fascinated, wide-eyed stare of a small animal caught by the hypnotic eyes of a predatory, swaying reptile.

Never before had she seen anything like this. Never before had she realized that a woman and a man could do the variety of things that the couple on the screen were doing.

She was going to be ill. She swallowed hard. Maybe the drinks were making her sick. But, more likely, it was the horrible picture.

Web pushed a glass into her hand. "Drink," he said.

"No ... I think I'm going to be ill."

"The drink will help."

She couldn't make her eyes leave the screen. Automatically she took the drink and swallowed it. The vodka was strangely tasteless, but she could feel it tingle and burn as she swallowed it. Maybe it would stop the nausea.

Was this what Tom wanted of her? What was happening on the screen? Was this love? It couldn't be!

A new thought frightened her. Would Web expect what they were witnessing?

Desperately she managed to shut her eyes. The vodka was making her dizzy. She thought back over the years. She remembered the marriage manuals she had read: the suggested experimentation and freedom from inhibitions; positions and techniques. But all of it had been only *words*. She never had visualized those things as she saw some of them on the screen. Nor had she ever allowed Tom to explore the more erotic potentials of the marriage bed.

Didn't anyone understand? Love-making—true love-making—was never forceful, always gentle—never demanding, always sharing—never a vigorous frenzy of abandon, always a fluid poem of sensation.

She opened her eyes again. The couple on the screen had become more intense in their efforts. The girl's face was contorted with emotion.

Animals fighting in a jungle, she thought.

Web took the glass from her hand.

"Altha, I don't know," he smiled crookedly, indicating the screen. "As they say—home was never like this."

Somehow she found a measure of relief in his words and half-embarrassed smile. Probably Web shared some of her feelings.

She said, "I hope you don't think I'm like that girl—I mean—"

"Of course not! And don't think I'm so—well ..."

"I know."

The drink had helped her, she thought. She felt much, much better. Sort of lightheaded, perhaps, and she wasn't quite so shocked by the couple on the screen. It didn't mean much now. The warm, pleasant, relaxing glow of the vodka was spreading through her. She giggled. She had not intended to giggle and it surprised her. Only she suddenly felt so *good*—so free and easy and pleasant and warm!

"They're so *uninhibited!*" she said. "So utterly *primitive!*"

She giggled again and Web chuckled with her. He finished his own drink and half-filled the glasses again.

"Let's have a nice time," he said, his voice a shade thick.

"Oh, yes—a real nice time. Not like up there, but really nice, Web?"

"Really nice."

"Web—I've never done anything like this before. Maybe I shouldn't?"

"Don't worry about it. Know what a lady writer said about it once? I mean, quote—sexual intercourse—unquote? She said it's the friendliest thing a man and woman can do together. That's what we'll be—friendly." He took a deep breath and exhaled. "Vodka's powerful," he said. "I feel no pain, Mrs. Gateson ... Altha ... nice name. Nice gal."

Tom Gateson felt as if he shouldn't be in the room, watching a dirty picture, sitting next to a woman not his wife, feeling her hands on him.

Despite the few escapades in school, the occasional call girls on business trips (actually they had resulted from too lavish entertainment by suppliers—and none of the experiences had been too satisfactory)—and despite the frank, hard sexual language Tom sometimes used with Altha, Tom Gateson knew a secret truth about himself: in the areas of bedroom adroitness, he talked a better game than he played.

The film he watched was having a confusing effect upon him, or possibly it was watching it with Maxine Vember next to him, her body close in unmistakable invitation.

Once before he had seen such a film at a stag party, but no women had been present. The male viewers had been raucous in their comments and boastful in their observations. The film had excited him. He had pictured himself enjoying such freedom with some unidentified, nebulous girl who would be completely co-operative.

This had been before his marriage. In the relatively few sexual episodes with girls before his marriage, there never had been anything like the things he had seen on the screen that night. Nor were there after marriage, nor during the relations that he and Altha had established before marriage.

He had suggested things to Altha during their brief premarriage affair. He had attempted a few unusual excursions, but she had refused to participate.

Their love-making usually took place on the back seat of his car, or on the sofa in her living room if they were certain her family was asleep. It had been simple, unimaginative and hurried. Biologically, it had been too effective when he had failed to take adequate precautions. The pregnancy had resulted.

Upon realizing that he and Altha would soon be married, he had promised himself that after marriage they would experiment and enjoy the full erotic scale of sexuality. Altha had intimated that it would be "different then."

But after marriage, and especially after the abortion, she had refused to participate in any but in the most routine and conventional manner. As Tom had tried to break through her reserve and attain a greater sexual rapport with her, she had withdrawn into a protective shell of reticence.

Tom was not quite certain why all this had come about, but he was very conscious of his frustrations.

He knew that he certainly was not "oversexed" in the accepted meaning of the description. The demands of his body were not abnormal. His sexual hunger was not excessive.

If there was a lack and a need, it was to accomplish and to know a complete fulfillment with Altha.

That was the goal he never seemed to achieve. Although he might manage his own physical fulfillment of the moment, he never managed to bring Altha to the soaring heights of mutual sharing that he longed to have with her.

Always there was the feeling of reserve; that he was doing nothing for her; never the masculine satisfaction of knowing that he had carried her into the ecstatic abandonment of the climax.

You don't do anything ...

Those were *his* words; *his* accusation; the blame he placed on her; the fault he found. Yet deep within him he sensed a truth. The failure might be his and not hers. A woman had to be *brought* to those soaring heights.

Eventually, in a perverse trend of reasoning, he found himself wondering if an experience between Altha and another man might not unlock the door to his own frustrations with her. Let another man cruelly break down the reserve. Let another man violate her sensitivities so that she would turn to her husband for devoted attention and fulfillment. And in doing this, might not he find a new experience for himself?

The thought stirred excitement in him when he was near Maxine Vember. He was certain that she had the wisdom of experience, and perhaps in such love-making he would find Altha.

As he watched the screen and felt Maxine Vember's exciting nearness, Tom thought of his relationships with his wife and their shortcomings. Tonight might change all of that. He picked up his drink.

"Don't drink too much, darling," Maxine said softly.

"When are we going?" he said.

"After the picture. There's usually a little milling around, but we'll leave soon."

"I'm ready now," he grinned.

The grin was bravado. Inwardly he remembered the trite phrase: "He talks a good game." He hoped he could more than talk a good game tonight with Maxine Vember. Somehow he keenly dreaded the thought of any possible failure with her.

Maxine had seen the movie. It was one of a dozen or so that Len had collected, paying exorbitant prices for them to a short, fat man who periodically appeared with a new offering.

Somewhere was a similar exhibit of her on such a film. This had been in the early days before she had graduated to the dubious status of being a call girl.

The film was photographed in a cheap Detroit hotel. Two young men had managed the photography. A third had been her partner on film. She had hated it, but she needed the fifty dollars they offered her.

She never had told Len about the incident, and when he bought new films she invariably had a few moments of uneasiness before she saw the latest acquisition. She wondered what she would say if he should ever—through a long chance—buy the film in which she appeared.

Otherwise, she frankly liked to watch the films. She had brazenly explained it to Len one night.

"Remember—it was my profession once, if you call it a profession. Techniques are important to a girl if she wants to make money. You don't come by all of them naturally. Some you have to learn. Above all you have to know how to act as if your John is really sending you. So I get a kick out of seeing how some of these girls work."

"That isn't the only kick you get out of the pictures," Len smiled wisely.

"I guess not," she admitted. "Maybe I'm about as close to being a nymph as you'll find these days."

"I wouldn't want it any different," he laughed.

He spoke the truth. It was this way between them. Len with his insatiable appetite, and she with hers. They were well mated in their hungers and ethics.

She knew of Len's activities with other women as well as he knew of her adultery with other men. However, despite their frequent and flagrant disdain for the marriage vows, they still found a basic attraction in one another, and almost invariably any detailed and clinical discussions of sexual matters ended in their own marriage bed with an intense exercise of their own lusts.

Maxine's need for sexual satisfaction seemed to have increased as she went into her thirties. Once it had been a frequent hunger. Now it had become an unreasonable and almost insuperable need. Sometimes it frightened her. What of the time when no man might be interested in her? The later years. When she had lost her looks—the well- formed body that so unfailingly enticed?

At such times her worry could easily become a panic that drove her to irrational actions. Then the necessity of having a man became an obsessive force that she could not combat.

There was the young magazine salesman. He had been frightened and awed by her woman's breasts and the vigor of her demanding body in the dim bedroom where she had drawn the shades on a summer afternoon.

There was the truck driver she had picked up in a roadside café one evening. He had followed her out to the parking area and they had driven a mile off the main highway on a side road in her car. His love-making had been more rape than love-making, except that her feverish, frantic acquiescence made it anything but rape.

In the last few years a more acceptible pattern had developed for Len and her. The key game was an excellent method of assuring a merry-go-round of partners.

Tonight would bring them new ones. In anticipation of the hours ahead, and in her perverted enjoyment of the film, Maxine pressed close against Tom Gateson. She knew that he was disturbed. His actual experience with women was probably far short of the impression he tried to convey, she thought. But he was young, and he appeared to be virile and eager. Possibly she could employ him to meet her own desire and hunger.

She watched the couple on the screen. They were not too experienced. The girl was less adept than she, Maxine, had been in the film years before.

Tom was displaying eagerness now. He had asked when they would leave. But she must be careful that he did not drink too much. Too many drinks could destroy his effectiveness, and she did not want this to happen.

Abruptly it was finished. The film was ended and Len was turning off the projector. He snapped a switch and soft light flooded the room. There was a rustle of movement, of laughs, of voices, and the clink of glasses.

The men were helping up the women from cushions. Len was starting the projector rewind.

"Anyone care for a repeat performance?" he smiled.

"I'll settle for the real thing," Web laughed.

"Vulgar," Altha said and giggled again.

Maxine pulled at Tom Gateson's hand. "Someone has to start," she announced. "Come on."

Web put an arm around Altha. "Ready?" he asked.

She nodded and within a few moments, and a trifle unsteadily, they followed Maxine and Tom outside to the parked cars.

Sarah finished her drink and watched the couples leave, observing Web with an odd detachment. Earlier in the evening Carl and Lillian had been at the first segment of the party with half a dozen other couples.

She and Carl had treated one another almost as if their afternoon at the lodge never had happened; evidenced only in the pressure of his hand against her waist as he stood by her for a few seconds, the unsaid words in a glance, and a brief moment when they had managed to be alone in the far shadows of the patio long enough for a quick, hard kiss.

"When?" he had asked.

"I don't know. I'll call you."

"You're not staying tonight, are you? Not for the afterparty games?"

"Web wants to."

"Sarah! Don't. I don't want you to—!"

"Don't ask me. Don't demand, Carl. I want no restrictions. I want to give as freely as I like. But I want freedom for myself, too."

"Not this after-party stuff, Sarah. I've never—Lillian nor I. And it's not—not in keeping with you!"

"But adultery was?" she had smiled wryly, thinking of their afternoon.

"Damn it, Sarah! I won't have you—"

"Carl, I'm sorry—I don't mean to antagonize you—nor disappoint you. No—nor to cheapen what's between us. It's simply that you must *not* try to demand things of me."

Now that the moment had arrived, Sarah remembered the disturbed, angry look in Carl's eyes and she wasn't realistically certain why she had agreed to play the key game this night.

She and Len listened to the two cars leave. Suddenly the house was very quiet. Len switched off some outside lights and turned to face her.

"Shall we?" he asked.

"Yes."

She walked across the room to him and he kissed her, long and deeply.

"We'll use one of the guest rooms," he said.

CHAPTER SIX

Web turned on the car radio for dance music from an all-night station. His drinks were hitting him hard and he was in a happy mood. His pairing off with Altha Gateson suddenly was a pleasant and wholly acceptable thing.

I should feel guilty, he thought. *But if I do, it's not because of Sarah, but because of Agnes! More faithful to my mistress than to my wife!*

Only Agnes probably wouldn't mind. Agnes isn't jealous. Agnes isn't possessive. Agnes and Altha ... Altha and Agnes. Both with a letter "A" and the scarlet letter "A" for adulteress!

He blinked his eyes and sought to regain a measure of sobriety. He had wandered to the wrong side of the street. He had to drive more carefully. He had to keep reasonably sober.

He tried to force the intoxication out of his mind. He began to do the multiplication tables mentally. Discipline. He needed discipline. Seven times eight is fifty-six. Eight times eight ...

He eased his foot on the gas and with concentrated effort drove a straight line near the right-hand curb of the deserted street. Automatically he made a turn. In a few moments they would be at the house.

"My bed," he said to himself. "Just for the perverse, stupid hell of it!"

Beside him in the car Altha quietly and smilingly listened to the music. Never before had she felt quite like this. Never had she drunk so much, nor felt the warm, pleasant tingling and laziness that she felt now.

The radio announcer did a commercial and then the music from *Never on Sunday* came from the speaker. She had seen the picture with Tom and she remembered the dance scene with the breaking glasses.

"That's how I feel," she told herself, "If I had glasses I'd break them! One, two, three, four ..."

She shut her eyes and hummed with the music.

I'm drunk, she thought. *Intoxicated. I don't like the word drunk. A girl should be intoxicated. Or high? Looped? Tingly? All the words, and I feel loose. A Loose Woman. Maybe they mean it like this. All loose and don't-caring. Not enough to pull down my dress and it's above my knees. All loose and don't-caring ...*

She hummed with the music and after a few seconds the car slowed and turned and came to a stop beside a house. She opened her eyes and looked at Web.

"You're not my husband," she giggled.

"I offer you my bed," he said solemnly and blinked.

"No more vodka, thank you."

"No more vodka. For you. For me. Come ..."

He reached across her and opened the car door on her side. She got out of the car and they met in the driveway behind the car. He took her arm and they walked a little unsteadily to the door of the house. Triumphantly he held up the house key she had selected earlier.

"The key that unlocks," he smiled.

He unlocked the door and they went in. He did not bother to turn on lights until he led her into a bedroom. He snapped a switch and soft bedside lamps came on.

Almost automatically, as if it was expected of them, they kissed and Web's fingers found a dress zipper and pulled. Altha giggled again.

"I drank too much," she said. "I feel so strange—as if nothing really mattered."

She shut her eyes and hummed the music she had been hearing as Web almost ritualistically undressed her. He led her to his bed. She sat on it and looked up at him, smiling, as if her thoughts were far away. She giggled again softly and lay back on the bed.

"So don't-caring," she said.

"That's nice," Web said indulgently.

"That's what we said," Altha smiled sleepily. "Nice. We'll keep it nice."

"Yes."

She shut her eyes and resumed her humming, her hands resting back, her lips softly smiling.

Web undressed without hurry, stopping once long enough to go to the kitchen and to return with two glasses and vodka. He poured slight drinks and persuaded Altha to sip hers and he gulped his.

He placed the glasses on a bedside table.

"This is my bed," he said seriously. "A very good bed." The drinks were hitting him again and he steadied himself as he stood by the bed table. He found the lamp switch and turned out the light. Almost immediately he turned the light on again.

"We don't mind the light," he said in a matter-of-fact voice.

On the bed beside Altha he turned her to him and they met in a kiss.

"Nice," Altha whispered. "You promised ..."

She shut her eyes and felt his hands upon her. Now it was beginning. This was the way it always began with Tom, and with this man—with this strange body which was in such close contact with hers—it was no different from the familiar, demanding movements and caresses of her husband.

Why didn't he just kiss and hold her first? Why wasn't he gentle with her? Why wasn't he different?

Masculine hands probed the protected secrets of her body. The tight clasp of fingers upon a breast made her gasp in pain. He was becoming more demanding. He was turning her so that his weight was heavy upon her, demanding surrender. Suddenly and instinctively she fought to keep herself closed and secure.

With an age-old, masculine prying movement of thighs and legs he forced her into open, helpless reception.

She tightly shut her eyes and for a few seconds she was nauseated with the drinks, the weight pressing down upon her, and the impending surrender.

She fought her confusion, trying to accept and rationalize what was happening. Perhaps just once, she told herself—just this once she could manage a complete surrender. Perhaps this man who was about to possess her would bring her the solace she sought. She would try. She would try almost objectively. She would transform this transgression into abandon; into a weapon to free herself of the all too familiar deadness that so frequently came over her in the midst of mounting excitement.

Tentatively she put her arms around him and pressed him to her. She would make herself do this. She would command herself to obey and succeed.

She felt the touch, the setting, and then the quick, intruding pain. In her hurt she convulsively tightened her arms and he mistook the gesture for pleasure and abandon. He whispered something unintelligible as he assaulted her with his demanding male vigor.

If she had known any excitement or stirring of desire, all of it was gone abruptly and completely. This was no different from what it was with Tom.

Frigidly, without emotion, pleasure or physical response, and with a functional acquiescence, and distaste, she waited for him to complete the act.

If Web noticed, he said nothing. He breathed hard and obviously the drinks had dulled his capabilities and possibly any skill that he had for the encounter. It was a matter-of-fact, slightly forced, uninspired performance that ended suddenly and almost mildly with significance only to him. Altha remained tense and unmoving until he was finished.

He rolled away from her and sighed, his eyes shut, the sleep of intoxication and satiation already descending upon him. Altha remained perfectly still, her knees drawn tightly together, her eyes shut in revulsion.

Nausea was forcing itself upward to her lips. Quickly and unsteadily she left the bed and found a bathroom, where she was ill.

Finally she felt a little better. She rinsed her mouth and drank some water. In a bathroom mirror she saw her naked shoulders and breasts. Again she felt revulsion, and now a deep shame. The alcohol in her system still made her unsteady.

She cleansed herself and used a bath towel from a rack. She carefully folded the towel and draped it over the side of the bathtub. She rinsed her mouth several times, and drank another half-glass of water.

When she returned to the bedroom Web was snoring, sprawled awkwardly and almost obscenely on the bed. Altha averted her eyes. She didn't want to think about it. She felt nothing but shame, disillusion and disgust. Nothing had come from it. No pleasure. No release. Only a disgusting, masculine-inspired, unsatisfactory, hopeless interlude that had left her soiled and dirtied by another man.

She dressed hurriedly. She saw the vodka and because the nausea was returning and had been stopped once before this night by the burning drink, she poured some into a glass and swallowed it quickly.

She had brought a small handbag. She found lipstick and applied it hurriedly, finding it a little difficult to stand steadily. She replaced the lipstick in the bag and checked to make certain that she had money.

In the living room she found a telephone and dialed for a taxi.

"Please send a cab," she said to the male voice that answered.

"Yes'm. Where?"

She realized that she didn't know the address. She knew the street, but not the number.

"Wait," she said. "Please wait just a minute...."

She put down the telephone and went to the door and stepped outside carefully leaving the door open. She read the house number and went back to the telephone. She gave the number to the dispatcher. "And please hurry," she said.

Fifteen minutes later she got out of a taxi and used her own key to let herself into her house. With a return of the disgusting and nauseated feeling she remembered that Tom and Maxine would be in the bedroom. She shuddered. She hated it. All of it. This night. Web. Maxine. Tom. Most of all she hated what men did to women.

She staggered a little as she made her way along a hallway. She felt dizzy from the drinks. She just wanted to find a bed, to lie down, to stop the world from whirling around. It was dark in the hallway. She wouldn't turn on the light.

Something was happening in her own bedroom. Something between Tom and Maxine, and damn Tom and what he wanted to do, and Maxine if she liked what Tom wanted to do! And Web for what he had done! And she, herself—Altha—for what *she* had done!'

"Whore," she whispered. "Whore!"

She found the door to the guest room and stumbled inside. Maybe they had used this room; not her bedroom. In the dim light she saw that the room was empty. It was all right. She was alone.

She undressed in the darkness, vaguely worrying about wrinkling the dress that she wore, and fell across the bed; nude, limp and almost immediately asleep.

A few moments later when Maxine quietly turned on a light by the bed, Altha stirred slightly, but she did not immediately awaken nor did she immediately feel the tentative, caressing touch of Maxine's hand upon her body.

CHAPTER SEVEN

A s Maxine Vember and Tom Gateson drove away from the Vember home Maxine sat close to Tom, slipping a hand beneath his arm so that she could obviously press against him.

"You didn't like the film," she observed.

"Did you?" he countered.

She laughed lightly. "They're one of Len's hobbies," she said, dismissing the subject. She moved against him. "Are you glad it's tonight?"

He nodded. "You know how I've been about you."

"It's working out as we planned."

"I hope you'll still think that a couple of hours from now," he smiled, a little dubiously.

The arrangements had been simple. At Maxine's suggestion he had placed a drop of transparent, fast-drying glue on his house key. When the moment came for the key drawing by the women, Maxine had insisted that the three husbands' house keys be placed in a hat to assure a blind drawing by the women. She had urged Altha to draw first. If Altha drew her husband's key the drawing would have to be repeated If not, Maxine—by drawing next—could quickly identify Tom's key by the invisible small dot of glue on the metal.

The plan had worked the first time, although Maxine was certain that Len knew that she had rigged the drawing—and was amused by the deception.

"You're still hesitant, Tom."

"No," he protested. "Those drinks—"

She shook her head. "Don't deny it. Don't apologize. You've never played the game before. The first time is always a little difficult in some ways. It's all so—well, it's so damned cut-and-dried adultery!"

"If you think I'm bothered about Altha ..."

"Actually you are," Maxine smiled. "And even a little excited about it. You're half-angry and jealous that she agreed to the whole thing. And somewhat excited that she did. You're even a little disgusted on all scores."

"I shouldn't be," he said. "I've had other women."

"And you're going to have me. Let's think about that! Do you want to talk about it?"

His subconscious worry crept into his mind. "I don't just *talk* a good game!" he grinned, denying his secret weakness.

"Then we'll play a good game," she laughed. "In just a little while."

She put a hand on him again and after a few seconds his foot pressed down on the gas.

"You raise hell with a man," he said.

"What are you going to do about it?"

"Plenty! Plenty!"

Later in the bedroom she began to undress. "Which is your bed?" she asked.

He nodded toward one of the twin beds. Without speaking, Maxine smiled and went to the other bed—Altha's—and stripped off the spread and a light blanket.

"It's warm, We won't need the blanket," she said.

He was looking at her and if he had been bothered about frustrations, guilts or any mental complexities of situation, all of it had disappeared in his contemplation of the woman by the bed.

Maxine knew how she appeared in his eyes. She had undressed until she wore only a brassiere and panties. She faced him and enjoyed the expression on his face and the intensity of his stare. In a typical feminine movement she reached behind and unhooked the brassiere and took it off. She had good breasts and knew it. She stood erect, proudly displaying herself for him, smiling at the growing excitement in his eyes. and his obvious flaring up of desire.

He stepped toward her and pulled her into his arms with a half-smothered exclamation. His mouth found hers. She responded to his kiss with all the skill born of her experience. One of his hands hooked into the elastic at her waist. She started to remonstrate and then shut her eyes and let him tear the fragile garment. It had been an expensive wisp of lace, but no garment was ever as satisfying to her as the kind of excitement she was arousing in Tom Gateson.

After a moment she squirmed free of his arms and gently pushed him away.

"Let's take showers," she whispered. "Then …" She left the rest of the thought to his imagination.

"And hurry!" he said. He glanced at the torn garment at her feet. "I'm sorry about that. I'll buy you something new."

He started to reach for her again, but she avoided him.

"The shower," she reminded him.

Within moments they stood together in a shower stall, the water cascading upon them as they soaped and lathered one another, feeling the slippery smoothness of wet, soaped skin.

They used towels hurriedly and went to the bedroom and Altha's bed that Maxine had selected. She remembered her thought earlier in the evening. She wanted to use Altha's bed. She liked the idea. She liked everything about adultery and the key game and the anticipation of a new man.

"Leave the light on," she said.

The sheets on the bed were clean and cool. She stretched luxuriously and waited for Tom to join her. He had gone to the kitchen for more drinks, although she had not encouraged him.

He came in with filled glasses and put them on a table between the twin beds. He offered her one, but she shook her head. He drank part of his, not taking his eyes from her.

She smiled in secret amusement. He had undressed but had put on a robe. Despite his eagerness for what was in store, he obviously was a little uneasy and felt the need of another drink to bolster his courage.

"Let the drink go," she said softly.

He put the glass down and after a brief hesitation he stood and took off the robe. He had the body of an athlete who had begun to soften and take on a little extra weight here and there. His shoulders were broad, solid and thick. His chest was deep. His thighs were solid, his legs powerful.

For a few seconds he self-consciously stood by the bed as she looked at him. She suspected that he was torn between a masculine vanity in his well-proportioned body and the embarrassment of the bedroom intimacy with a woman other than his wife.

"Come here," she said.

He bent over her and she put her arms around his neck and pulled him down. After a moment she pushed her hands against his chest in gentle repulsion.

"No ... not yet. There's no hurry, darling. Let me show you...."

At first his eagerness was an impatient, troublesome hindrance. After moments the skill of her practiced caresses seemed almost to immobilize him in a trembling tenseness. He moaned and she moved her hands again and sought him with her lips.

"Now," he said his voice suddenly urgent. "Now—I can't wait longer—"

"But, darling—we're just starting," she whispered.

"You're driving me crazy with that. Let me have you—*please!*"

"All right," she smiled soothingly. She moved to accommodate him and she whispered again, "Now, Tom ... all right ... now!"

Then for a brief moment she tried to stop him, to control his undisciplined, frantic union with her. She knew it was useless after seconds and she tried to share it with him in her own self-indulgence, but he was too fast for her and she cursed to herself in angry frustration.

Afterward he was an exhausted, clumsy weight upon her while the futility of her unquenched desire seemed to shriek within her. She kept the words of anger and disappointment from her lips. She knew from experience that she still might salvage something of the night for herself.

"I'm sorry," he finally said. "I mean about you—"

"It's all right," she said, trying to conceal her disappointment. She moved to let him know that she wanted him away from her for the moment. "It wasn't your fault."

He pushed himself up and away from her.

"Maybe a little later," he said apologetically.

"Why don't you sleep a while?" she said. *What else is there is say?* she thought. *He's inexperienced—a boy.*

He left the bed and finished his drink.

"Maybe if you'd help me a little ..." he suggested hopefully.

She shook her head. "Not yet. It wouldn't do any good for a while. Maybe if you slept—and no more drinks?"

"Sure. That's probably what was wrong. The drinks." He smiled unconvincingly, glad to find an excuse for an inept performance.

She smiled. "Darling, stretch out and try to sleep. That'll help most."

With amusement she watched him get into the robe again before he stretched out on his own bed. The modesty of inexperience, she thought.

"I'll be back in a few moments," she said. She left the bedroom and went into the bathroom. When she returned Tom was asleep.

The room was warm. She found a package of cigarettes on a dresser where he had methodically unloaded his pockets as he had undressed. She lit a cigarette and returned to the bed and propped up a pillow. After a moment she turned out the light. She wasn't sleepy. She could risk smoking in bed. She could never sleep the way she felt now. Every nerve in her body seemed to be taut. Her desire was fully awakened, unreasonable and harsh in its demands.

She glanced at the other bed in the dimness of the room. He had been a disappointment. He had served only to fan the fires that tormented her so frequently. He had given her no peace, no escape, no release, and now she would have to wait until he had rested. She knew his type only too well. Unfortunately you never knew for sure until you had been with them once.

She remembered the years and the men; the professional football player who had been wholly inadequate in bed; the small, thin gambler who had brought her ecstasies she seldom had experienced. You never knew. You couldn't know by just looking at them. And now she had to wait, and even if she waited she couldn't be certain. He probably was another victim of the virtual impotency that so many men suffered; the "premature" problem, the lack of control and the inadequacy of skill.

Also, she suspected, Tom was very inexperienced. Her caresses had brought almost a frantic response that a more experienced man might not have displayed. Idly she wondered if Altha was frigid.

Some of Tom Gateson's behavior might indicate that his desire for an episode in adultery might be the result of marital frustrations. How frequently she had seen similar instances when she had worked as a call girl! The sexually unhappy, disappointed, seeking businessmen who had come to her when the denials and frigidity of unresponsive wives had driven them to a responsive satisfactory woman.

"So," she said to herself. "So maybe that's it. Only Altha has *something*—undoubtedly *something*. Maybe he can't reach her. Maybe he doesn't know. There's so much he doesn't understand."

Well, she would wait a half-hour or so. Let Tom sleep. Possibly something still could be salvaged of the night.

Quietly she smoked and waited, letting her thoughts drift. She finished a second and then a third cigarette. She was about to awaken the sleeping man when she heard a car stop in front. A car door slammed and the car drove away.

Faintly she heard the sound of a key in the lock and the door being unlocked. Someone moved in the hallway, past the door. Another door opened and was closed.

She was certain that Altha had come home. She wondered what had happened between Altha and Web. Whatever had happened, it hadn't lasted long and probably not to Altha's pleasure. She probably had come home in a taxi alone. Web would have seen her to the door, at least.

Maxine smiled in the darkness. Carefully she put out the cigarette in an ash tray and after a while she left the bed and stepped into the hallway, quietly closing the bedroom door behind her. Suddenly she knew what she wanted. Now desires and excitement coursed through her as she recognized the possibility of this unexpected opportunity.

She opened the next door in the hallway. She looked into a guest bedroom and saw the nude figure on the bed, and heard Altha's soft breathing as she slept.

Quietly Maxine crossed the room to the bed. She groped at a bedside lamp and turned on the light. For a long moment she stared silently at the young, sleeping woman, seeing the perfection of naked breasts, the gentle curve of hips and thighs, the darkened shadow of the groin, the softness of skin, the sheen of hair, the fullness of lips.

She sat on the bed beside the sleeping woman, and after a few moments of contemplating the pretty face and the lovely body she reached out a caressing hand.

Altha stirred in her sleep and Maxine stopped the gentle stroking. Seconds later she resumed it and a few moments later Altha opened her eyes. She looked startled and raised up to rest on one elbow.

"What ...? Oh ... Maxine!" She sank back on the bed. Maxine had removed her hand. She smiled at Altha.

"Are you all right?" she asked.

"Yes ... yes, I think so. I had so many drinks. I'm still ... tight, I guess. Dizzy. I couldn't stay there with him."

"I know."

"It wasn't—I mean, it didn't work out like I thought it would and ..." Altha suddenly smiled. "Do you know what I'm talking about Maxine?"

"Of course. Men. They don't understand. Let me show you. They don't understand gentleness like this ..." She resumed her careful stroking of Altha's soft flesh, temporarily selecting the less intimate erogenous areas of Altha's body for her ministrations. "I love to massage," she said. Somehow her words seemed to give them a rationalization for what she was doing. "Isn't it soothing?"

Altha nodded and shut her eyes again. Gradually she stirred a little under Maxine's hand.

"You have a beautiful body," Maxine whispered, her caresses becoming bolder. "I doubt if any man could appreciate it, or know how to treat it."

Under Maxine's soft, insistent hands Altha felt herself relax. A pleasant feeling of anticipation and enjoyment seemed to creep through her. She liked the soothing hands; the experienced woman hands that knew the secret places; the gentle hands; the knowing hands that hardly touched, yet stroked so softly and knowingly.

The sense of expectation and pleasure mounted in her and she felt new, strange desires. She kept her eyes tightly closed and tried to believe that it was not happening, that it was a dream.

When she felt Maxine's lips upon her, and the first kiss, she shuddered, but it was with a new, intense pleasure such as she never had experienced before.

"Let me teach you," Maxine whispered.

The heady drinks Altha had taken were still with her. The strange hands and the knowing lips and mouth were a strange, exciting, desirable sacrilege that violated the things she had been taught and believed.

She had heard and read about the relationships that could exist between women, but the knowledge was vague and almost academic. Never before had she allowed another woman to touch her like this, nor to kiss her like this.

There had been the girl at the university who had attracted her so much, and there had been the casual touching and school-girl kisses that were supposed to be a girl-to-girl thing, but always had carried an overtone of too much pleasure in the contact, but nothing had come of it.

And she had read what she could find about lesbianism. She even had recognized her own unusual and provocative interest in it, but she never had wholly identified herself with an active participation in the deviation.

But it was happening to her now as she had read about it in the books on abnormal psychology, in the case histories she had found in some of the books. She actively was participating in a lesbian relationship. The sensations that seemed at the moment to be exquisite, the new subtleties of hands and lips upon her body, the mounting fervor toward compulsive desire, the response, the yearning for climactic achievement, were real and breath-taking.

This was what she had expected and had never experienced with Tom, nor with Web. This was the way it was supposed to be. This was sweet deliverance.

Maxine now had transcended the pretense of massage, and the preliminaries of seduction.

"Teach me," Altha murmured breathlessly. "Teach me ... teach me, Maxine ... I want to know."

"Yes, darling ... like this ... and this ... and this ..." Maxine demonstrated her experienced techniques with caressess that became increasingly daring.

"Oh, yes ..." Altha whispered. "Yes ... yes ... yes ..."

She moved in uninhibited response and Maxine possessed her in the profane rites of the cult. Her own excitement was evident in her feverish increase of rhythm. In the bold way she pressed her naked body against Altha's yielding, quivering flesh.

Altha threw her head back and bit her lower lip in an ecstasy that was touched with an almost unbearable thread of exhausting, delicate pain.

For one brief instant, with eyes closed, she groped with her hands to stop the caresses, and then her hands fell back listlessly, and she gave herself up completely to sensation, until finally she wept in the excruciating abandon of the moment.

CHAPTER EIGHT

Len Vember touched a light switch and smiled as he watched Sarah look around the room.

"We call it a guest room," he said. "Actually it's as large as the master bedroom. I sometimes sleep here, and it serves as more than a bedroom." He indicated a bookcase, a hi-fi stereo cabinet, easy lounging chairs, a chaise longe. It was a spacious, sprawling room and it held a wide, oversize bed. An open door permitted a glimpse into a bathroom with a sunken tub.

Colors in the room were subtle, the lighting was soft, and when Vember went to the phonograph and turned it on, music quietly filled the room. He opened a cabinet and indicated bottles and glasses.

"Drink?"

She shook her head. "No. I've had enough. This is a lovely room, Len. Really, it is."

He smiled. "I like the de luxe—cars, homes ... and women," he said. He went to the bed and stripped back a rich, decorator's spread and she saw that the sheets were black silk. Len shrugged. "Why not?" he said. "The more luxurious the setting, the better the play!"

She laughed a little. "I'm not sure, Len ..."

He laughed with her. "I know. But you'll enjoy it. I promise you that. Come here."

She crossed the deep, rich, wall-to-wall carpeting as he led her to one of two closed doors. He opened one and a light automatically came on. She looked into a spacious dressing room, lined on one side with sliding closet doors.

Len slid back one of the doors and took a black, silk robe from a hanger and gave it to her. He opened a drawer next to the floor and brought out cellophane-wrapped, straw guest slippers obviously Orientally designed and manufactured for a feminine foot. He indicated a dressing table and picked up an expensive-appearing vial of perfume.

"Mind?" he said. "It's my favorite for a beautiful woman."

"Len, you—I mean … !" She laughed softly.

He shared her amusement again. "I know, Sarah. I make a production of it. But with you it should be a production, and I was hoping it *would* be you. Very much so."

"Thank you, Len—I *suppose* I should thank you."

"For telling you that you're beautiful and desirable?" He shook his head and put an arm around her and kissed her.

"This door opens to the bath," he said. He opened the connecting door. "I'll leave you to privacy. When you're ready I'll be waiting."

He left her and she had a sudden impulse to laugh again. She hadn't realized that a man like Len could take seduction or adultery or love-making so seriously! This was a far, far cry from a hot, small bedroom in a summer cabin in the mountains!

The brief comparison and memory made her think of Carl. She was about to go to bed with another man, the second act of unfaithfulness upon her part, yet the memory of the afternoon with Carl was strong and she found herself wishing that Carl would be waiting for her in the large room—not Len.

She undressed slowly, staring at herself in a full-length mirror, suddenly very conscious of her body. She had sunned frequently on their patio, and she often had worn a bikini, with only a wispy excuse of a halter, the narrow, curved bands of white skin against the tan served only to accent the definition of her womanhood.

Somewhere in the house she heard water running. Undoubtedly there were other bathrooms and she sensed that Len probably was taking a quick shower. Impulsively she went into the adjacent bathroom.

She showered quickly and dried herself with a large, enveloping towel. Back in the dressing room she quickly slipped into the black robe that offered transparant enticement rather than concealment. She broke the cellophane wrapping on the slippers and put them on.

She remembered the perfume and smiled again. Len overlooked nothing. She opened the vial. The scent was subtle and exciting. She understood why he liked it. She touched it sparingly at her body, not neglecting her breasts.

A new comb was in its transparent wrapper. She stripped away the wrapping and combed her hair. She sat at the dressing table and used lipstick. Then, satisfied with her appearance, she arose and walked into the room.

Len was waiting. He wore a heavy, black silk robe that was as opaque as hers was transparent, contrasting almost handsomely with his gray hair. His inscrutable dark eyes swept her body with a quick, appraising look.

"You *are* beautiful," he said. "Summer tan and golden hair!"

He was standing by the liquor cabinet, busy with some small task. She did not recognize the pulsating music from the phonograph, but it was low and remarkably clear in its high fidelity offering. There was a primitive, elemental quality in its rhythm and theme.

He came to her and offered her a glass. "You'll like this," he said. "Brandy—imported and strong. Very strong."

The liquor had a pungent taste and she knew it would be heady and relaxing. She drank slowly.

"Like it?" he asked.

"Yes, but only a little of it. It *is* strong."

"Very," he nodded.

"You really didn't need it," she smiled. "I don't have to be seduced. I'm willing."

"It's not for easy seduction. It's for uninhibited readiness," he said, his eyes showing his amusement.

He took her empty glass and returned it with his own to the cabinet. He touched a controlling switch on the wall and the lights became softer. The music seemed to be more accented by the lowered lights.

Sarah stood almost in the center of the room. Suddenly she hoped that there would be no more stage setting. A little more of the music would be a touch too much. A little more cleverness with soft lights would be too theatrical. Another unidentified, strong drink would be too obvious, and she already was not certain that she liked the black robe, and especially the black sheets. She could vizualize their contrasting bodies against the blackness and the thought was slightly repulsive.

I guess I'm just a healthy, American, female type, she thought. *I wasn't made for seraglios.*

Furthermore, she realized, she didn't want to participate in a theatrical production written to be played by two in a bedroom especially equipped for assignation.

"Len," she said, with sudden conviction. He turned to look at her with a questioning expression in his dark eyes. "Let's not overdo it," she said.

He shrugged. "If you'd rather not—"

"No. I don't want to back out. But we're here for a particular reason and … well, let's just get on with it."

"All right." Apparently he understood her mood. He smiled. "Unfasten your robe, and let it drop to the floor. That's a logical beginning."

"Yes, I think it is," she said. She had asked for it, and now the next move was up to her. She unfastened the robe and let it drop to the floor. A little embarrassed, she stood in the nude for him.

"You're lovely," he said quietly. "Really beautiful."

"Not *that* good-looking, Len," she said flatly. "I'm past thirty. A woman knows."

"A woman doesn't know. Not what a man may like."

"What do you want me to do?" she asked, almost defiantly. Her embarrassment was growing.

"The natural thing under the circumstances. Walk over to the bed."

"That's natural enough under the circumstances!" she smiled. "Only I'm feeling terribly self-conscious."

"Don't you feel that last drink? It should help a little!" He was smiling with her, sharing the moment, at ease.

"I probably wouldn't be quite so bold if I didn't," she admitted. She did feel the drink, and it was relaxing her.

"We're doing a lot of talking," he said. He was coming toward her as she walked to the bed. She sat down on the edge of the bed and abruptly she didn't know how to gracefully lie back for him.

"I feel like a whore," she said softly.

"You might be a mistress, or a concubine, or an obedient wife—but I doubt if you could be a whore. I don't think you could be promiscuous enough. But you might try feeling like a whore for the excitement. Maybe it would make it easier."

"What would a whore do under the circumstances?"

"Simply lie back and offer her wares."

She shuddered a little. "You make it sound commercial."

"For a whore it *is* commercial."

"Then how would a mistress or concubine act?"

"The same way, if that's what her lover wanted."

"What do *you* want *me* to do?"

He took off his black robe and draped it over a near-by chair. His tanned body was trimly muscled and he moved with an animal grace. He stood with his back to her and said: "Now is a good time for you to lie back. If I'm not watching, it won't bother you. Lie back, then shut your eyes and all you'll have to do is wait. I'll do all the rest."

"Why not?" she said, trying to say the words lightly.

She stretched out on the bed, unexpectedly pleased by the feel of the silk sheet, and conscious that her tanned body with the two white bands, was flatteringly outlined against the yet black. Maybe Len had a thing in his stage productions! She shut her eyes. The drink was much headier than she had suspected.

She felt his weight upon the bed as he sat by her, and although her eyes were closed, she knew that he was looking at her. She waited. A feeling of expectancy and uncertainty crept through her. A strangely pleasant uneasiness fluttered along her nervous system. She kept her eyes tightly closed and wondered where he would touch her first, what he would do, what was going to happen.

Then, oddly, she was back to the first times with Harold, her brother, and the same waiting and expectancy, the same excited wondering about the unknown.

Abruptly the suspense was broken, and in an odd, startling way that she had not anticipated. She felt a shift of his weight upon the bed. Almost breathlessly she waited his touch. Then with a startling stab of sensory pleasure she felt his kiss the ultra-sensitive softness of an instep. Seconds later she felt his hands begin their exploration of her thighs.

He moved again and the weight shifted. She opened her eyes and he was bending over her. Her lips parted in excitement and invitation, but his dark eyes held hers only for seconds. Smiling he ignored her waiting lips and his mouth gently found a breast. She gasped ecstatically.

Now began for Sarah a new world of sexuality that was beyond any heights of sensation and desire that she ever had experienced.

Only days previously, the first barrier had been broken when the boredom and frustrations of marriage with Web had thrown her into the arms of Carl Trojan. With the breaking of the marriage vow there also had been the breaking of long-observed restrictions. Now, after the first violation, the second was easier. After the first taste of the forbidden, the second was more enticing. After the first short journey into the unknown, the desire for another exploration was more welcome.

She deliberately had courted this second experience by agreeing to play the key game. The reasons for that agreement she understood. She was tired of marriage with Web. She was laden with frustration and desires that were unsatisfied. She was sick and tired of being the wife of a man who went to bed with another woman, who had lived with the other woman—smooth blond Agnes Aiten—before his marriage with Sarah, and had returned to the other woman after the marriage. Sarah had seen them together, recognized the "working late" excuses with other small damning evidences; lipstick stains, the perfume Agnes used, and all the rest.

Despite the rationalizations that Sarah might have built to justify her new turn in behavior, tonight's episode was undoubtedly—and consciously—made easier by the drinks she had freely accepted. With each one it seemed that more inhibitions and misgivings faded away. Even if she recognized the dangers and the moral degradation for those who played the game of bedroom lottery, the drinks helped to make them unimportant at the moment.

Now—ten minutes or so after Len Vember had first kissed the instep of her right foot and brought a small, responsive quiver along her thigh and leg—she realized vaguely that she had plunged more deeply into the unexplored byways and dark shadows of sensuality than she had ever known before.

Len had brought her to these depths, or heights, skillfully and quickly. His lips and hands had violated her as no man ever had violated her in caress and demand.

The heights of passion and desire that she had reached with Carl were now transcended by the devastating, shuddering, excruciating waves of sensuality and sensory fire that made her body a moving, demanding, seeking entity in itself.

Why didn't he go on? Why didn't he finish it? Why didn't he consummate it?

She clutched at him and demanded with her most primitive invitation of body and movement. She bit at him and her nails sank into his skin.

At the moment when she thought she could bear it no longer; when she felt an inward screaming of nerves as they sought release; when she wept in a strange, painful agony of desire—at that moment he took her and her response was immediate, primitive, elemental and female.

Afterward she could hardly remember how it had been in those mad, skillfully sustained moments. Len Vember deliberately took her into a new world she had never known before; brought her skillfully and certainly to her moaning cry of abandon, to her ecstasy, to build it again to the same keening heights, and the cry of fulfillment, and the released limpness.

Finally there was a last harsh and painful moment when his hands were vices upon her, and pleasure was also pain. She suffered him in his own release. It was far too late to bring more ecstasy to her. She could suffer him, and be helplessly used.

She must have fainted. He no longer was the driving, violent captor desecrating the temples of her body. She was alone on the silk and she felt the faint coolness of unrestricted air upon her skin.

Again she recognized his weight upon the side of the bed. A hand slipped under her neck and an arm to support and half-raised her.

"You're wonderful," Len's voice said. "You—!" He held something to her lips. "Here … drink it. You need some brandy. It was rough!"

Automatically and obediently, because it was too much trouble to resist, she swallowed the brandy. It burned and after a few seconds she liked the pleasant warmth it spread through her. Strength returned and she opened her eyes.

"I must have fainted," she said.

"And slept," Len told her. "I've never had anyone like you. Was it that good for you?"

She managed a smile. "Need you ask?"

"There's more."

"I don't believe I could stand it, Len. Truly."

"We'll see."

"What more *could* there be?"

The drink was beginning to take greater effect. A pleasant lassitude and feeling of acceptance was spreading through her like sunshine into a darkened corner. Maybe there *was* more. Maybe Len had more to bring her in the new world

"What's more?" she asked again, smiling.

"First another drink," he said.

He brought the glass to her and another for himself. They drank quickly and as they drank Len put his free hand upon her and began the slow stimulation of gentle caresses.

Despite her exhaustion, and the slight feeling of unreality that the drinks were building in her, she liked the feel of his hand and the first small reawakening of sensation began again, slowly building into the stirring of desire.

Once again he began his love-making, only this time she vaguely sensed a change in him. His hands had become rougher. His kisses were harsh and more demanding. At first the change brought a new response in her. Despite the pain and roughness, there also was pleasure and excitement. The second strong drink was making her dizzy and she shut her eyes and hung on to Len for a moment.

"What more?" she asked again, not fully understanding why she asked the question, or why there could be more; or more of *what?*

"I'll show you," he whispered. "Turn over." He drew away from her and turned her so that she lay face down. Then he left her and she shut her eyes, befuddled, not certain why she was stretched out this way on the bed, suddenly sleepy, and very dizzy.

She sensed that Len was back at the bedside, standing above her.

"Now I'll show you, Sarah," he said tightly. "You want more—now there'll be more. *You'll do as I say. You'll do as I say, you rutting bitch!*"

She could not see his arm go up, nor the length of leather belt that hung in a lazy loop from his hand as he began the downward snap. When the leather cut into her back she screamed.

Desperately she tried to get up from the bed. A hand violently pushed her down. The leather burned into her tender skin.

She screamed again and fought to break away. The belt lashed and cracked and the tempo of the lashes increased.

Len breathed hard. His only voice was a low, animallike growl as he put his strength to the mad cadence of his whip.

Finally she was off the bed, crawling, trying to get away from the man and the searing, ruthless leather. Her hands found a table and she pulled herself up. A whip of the lash came high and curled around a cheek and she felt the pain of a split lip. The leather curled around her loins, whipped across her back to tender breasts.

Blindly her hands sought something—anything—to use in defense. Her fingers closed around the thin rod of a heavy, brass-shaded desk lamp on the table. She jerked at it and felt the connecting cord hold and then break free.

The leather lashed across her back again. Len was speaking now in harsh, simple expletives and words of pleasure.

She turned and raised the heavy lamp and brought it down as hard as she could on Len's head. She saw his expression of surprise, and then the blankness that came over his face. He stumbled back and then fell to the floor. The leather belt slipped from his limp fingers.

Sickness swept in a wave over Sarah. She reeled and tried to steady herself at the table where she had found the lamp. She had to get out, she thought. Before Len got up again. He was already moving. She hadn't killed him. He was breathing. He was groping with one hand.

If only she hadn't drunk so much. She felt drunk. She was dizzy and unsteady and everything was unreal. Only the pain on her back—the smarting, burning pain—was real. By the bed she saw the slippers she had worn. She ought to put on slippers if she left.

She shook her head, trying to clear her mind. *I drank too much. I'm going to be sick. I have to get out. I must put on the slippers.*

She stumbled to the bed and managed to shove her feet into the straw slippers. She looked down at her naked body. The belt-whip had raised two ugly welts across her breasts. It was all a nightmare.

"Get out," she said aloud. "Run … run!" She needed something to cover her nakedness.

She saw the black robe on the chair near the bed. She saw the robe she had dropped on the floor. *So thin,* she thought. *I can't wear that.* She went to the chair and put on the heavy black silk robe that Len Vember had worn. She belted it, tying the knot a little off-center and a few inches below the letter "V" embroidered in scarlet upon the black silk. At that moment Len Vember spoke in a thick voice.

"Damn you … I'll … fix you. But—good!"

Sarah looked at him in alarm. He was trying to get to his hands and knees, but he was having trouble. He sank down again and rested, breathing heavily.

"Get out," she whispered to herself. "Get out." She ran from the room and down a hallway. She crossed through the darkened living room. Behind her something crashed. She had to get out. Fast … fast … fast! She didn't know what he would do now. He was like a crazy man. She didn't know.

She fought to keep from being sick as she struggled to find the combination of the bolted lock on the front door. The knob turned in her hand and finally when she turned a bolt, the door opened.

She ran from the house into the darkness, across dew-covered grass that wet the straw slippers, to a driveway and across black asphalt.

Moments later she stopped and gasped for breath. High hedges lined both sides of deserted residential streets. She listened and heard no footsteps. There was only the small night sounds and the sleeping city. She was away from a major street in an area of curving drives.

She walked. There were no lighted windows. She saw no one, heard no one. She didn't know where she was, and now the alcohol was blending with the pain of the whipping so that she was dazed.

Once or twice she talked, incoherently. But she kept on walking, stumbling occasionally, and even staggering when the waves of dizziness came over her. Once she stopped and looked back listening. She saw no one. She heard no footsteps following her. She turned and went on, stumbling a trifle in her flight.

The car came upon her suddenly, turning a corner, its lights sweeping across her, and then stopping with a slight screech of brakes.

It was an old car that had seen too many miles and rough abuse. Inside the car five youths looked at the woman held by the full glare of the headlights.

"Like crazy," the driver said. "Like crazy, man!"

The five got out of the car and crossed the street. Sarah watched them approach, too dazed to understand fully what was happening. She stood quietly in the light, swaying slightly, staring into the brightness, trying to see into the blackness beyond.

The five young men crowded around her. They had been drinking all night. They were without women. Three of them had records at the city police station. The other two would have had records if they had been caught. All of them had stolen many times. All of them had been guilty of seduction; four had been guilty of rape, but had never been accused or caught; the other was willing. He was only sixteen, the others ranged from seventeen to twenty-two. The newspapers talked about them as the "delinquent problem." Some of the more knowledgeable and hard-pressed city officials and newspaper workers called them "those goddamned punks." They had earned the description.

Now they stood around Sarah Emmlin and stared at her.

Suddenly Sarah was frightened. She wished her mind were clear. She almost wished she were back in the house with Len. She pulled the robe close around her.

One of the youths reached out, pulled the knot loose, and in a quick stripping movement opened the robe wide.

He stepped to one side and the others separated so that the glare of the headlights were full upon her nude body.

"Let's make it!" one of the youths said. "Man! Out on that back road!"

"Like crazy!" the driver said. He reached out and his hand squeezed hard on one of Sarah's bared breasts. She screamed and he quickly clamped his other hand over her mouth.

In seconds they had picked her up and carried her to the car. They threw her into the back seat and three of the youths got in with her. The driver started the car with a gunned engine and another screech of tires. In the back seat Sarah wept, fought, bit and tried to scream against the obscene indignities of six hands upon her unprotected body.

Later, when they had mauled and abused her naked flesh and spent the violence of their passion upon her, they left her on a patch of trampled field, a few yards from a back road in surburban woods and brush, and a mile from the nearest farmhouse.

The first gray of a false dawn was spreading across the landscape as their car bumped over the unpaved turn-off until it came to an asphalt highway and sped away toward the city.

Sarah lay sobbing convulsively on the grass. Underneath her back a twig or small stone pressed into her naked skin. It was just another pain to endure. She felt as if there was agony everywhere in her body. It was almost too painful to move, to try to get up, even to roll over on her side.

The preceding hour was both clear and confused in her mind. The indignities were clearly defined and remembered, but not in sequence nor identified with any one of the youths. They had held her down, hands on wrists and ankles while the grass and twigs and small stones were painful against the seared, inflamed skin of her back where the belt had lashed it.

She had struggled and tried to scream. She had tried to bite a hand over her mouth; to twist away from the grasping, feeling uncouth touch of strange and rapacious hands.

That came in the first moments. Then the first rape. After that the others. She didn't know how many times. She couldn't remember that, nor could she remember the individual, separate indignities forced upon her. But she remembered the pain and some of the obscene words; the biting mouths; the hot, fetid odors of their breathing in her nostrils; and the driving, bruising, tearing force of violation.

She tried to stop remembering what was left, and desperately sought a reserve strength that might overcome her aching exhaustion. After moments she managed to roll to her side, and then face down. She struggled to her hands and knees and stared at the ground a few inches from her face.

Small, dark drops settled on the flattened grass in the gray light. She ran her tongue over her lips. They were cut and swollen. She tasted blood.

After a very long time—it must have been a very long time, she thought—she pushed herself up to a kneeling position. She looked about her. The black robe was on the ground. It was ripped a little at one shoulder where they had torn it from her.

Gritting her teeth against pain, she stood and retrieved the robe and draped it around her. The straw slippers were not in sight. Barefooted she walked carefully along the short stretch of unpaved road out of the underbrush to the secondary highway. No traffic passed. Somewhere a dog barked. It was getting light and it was chilly with the bite of dawn.

She hesitated when she reached the asphalt. She was not sure which way she should walk. It didn't make much difference, she thought. She turned right and began to walk in a tired, slightly unsteady gait. The pavement hurt her feet. Her back hurt. There was a raw, burning sensation in the area of her pelvis.

A car came toward her. For a moment she almost ran into the brush at the side of the road. Fright had become a real, terrible thing born of experience.

The car was a truck. She could see the cab and the heavy grillework and bumper. The body of the truck stuck out at the sides; not a large, over-the-road type of truck that she had met frequently on the main highways, but a smaller truck such as farmers used.

She stopped walking and stood at the side of the road and watched the truck approach her. It was difficult for her to think. She would have to say something if the driver stopped. She didn't know what to say. She wrapped the black robe closer about her.

The truck slowed and stopped and a man stared at her. He was a middle-aged man with a very tanned face. He wore no hat, and his hair was iron-gray. He wore a work shirt, open at the neck. The truck had no sides and it was not loaded.

"Hello," the man said. He had a deep, full voice. He was frowning as he stared at her. The greeting sounded strange to her. It didn't seem as if he should just say, "Hello."

Possibly the man felt that the greeting was inadequate or not in keeping with the situation. He shook his head a little, and appeared to be genuinely concerned, or startled. The frown deepened.

"Are you in trouble, lady?" he asked.

She nodded. "Yes." Now her voice sounded as inadequate as his first greeting had been. "Yes," she said again. "Can you help me?"

"I live back the road a mile or so, lady. I think I'd better take you there. I want the missus in this—I mean, I don't want anyone to think that I—"

"I understand," Sarah said. She ran her tongue over her cut lips and tasted blood again. "I need help. I need a doctor—"

"Sure. I think I know what you mean. Some man did this?"

"*Men*," Sarah said. She was becoming faint and the man's face was blurring. Her hands helplessly dropped to her sides. She was going to fall and she couldn't do anything about it. Instinctively she fought the engulfing darkness.

The robe swung open and revealed her body. The man in the truck saw the welts where the belt had circled over and beneath her breasts. He saw the evidences of maltreatment, manhandling and rape.

"Christ!" he said. He opened the car door and swung down to the pavement. Sarah had crumpled into unconsciousness and lay on the asphalt.

The man picked her up and carried her around the truck to put her on the wide seat, where she slumped limply, the robe trailing away from her to the floor of the cab. He looked at her woman's body, his face expressionless. He pulled the robe over her and for just a second one of his large hands firmly cupped a breast. Quickly he took the hand away and swore under his breath, ashamed of the unexpected impulse and angry with himself for obeying it.

He walked around the truck, lighting a cigarette and inhaling deeply.

He swore again, in a sort of self-chastisement, and climbed into the truck. He backed and turned. A few moments later he drove into a yard by a large, modern farmhouse. He got out of the truck and went in the back door.

"Alice!" he called.

A pleasant-appearing, middle-aged woman came from the front of the house.

"What's wrong, Jim? I saw you turn in. You look sort of strange! … *What happened?*"

"A woman. She was down the road."

"Jim! You didn't hit her with the car! There wasn't an accident?" Alarm was in the woman's voice.

"No. She was walking this way. You better go out, Alice. She's in the truck. You'll see. I think she's been hurt."

"It must have been a car accident! You'd better call the sheriff's office—"

"After we get her in here. It wasn't a car accident, Alice. Not what happened to *her!*"

"What did happen to her?" The woman glanced curiously at her husband as they hurried from the house toward the truck.

His expression was hard and his lips looked thin. "Rape," he said tightly. "And God knows what else!"

PART III

THE LOSERS

CHAPTER NINE

At 6:30 A.M. Kindrake Smith, a reporter on the *Ledger,* ordinarily would not be sitting in Emergency Admittance in City General Hospital talking with Dr. T. D. Jimson, a resident physician on duty.

The *Ledger* was a morning paper. Its staff worked at night, for the greater part. During the previous night—shortly before midnight and just before the presses started to roll for the following morning's editions—a four-alarm fire broke loose in a disreputable hotel in the seamier part of Douglas City.

The fire had been spectacular. No lives had been lost, but several firemen had been injured. Smith had covered the fire. He had phoned in his story to rewrite and had sent a photographer scurrying back to the paper with pictures to cover as much as possible in the early editions.

The fire had been difficult to control and it was after 5:00 A.M. before most of the excitement was over. Smith had stopped for ham and eggs and coffee and then had decided to look in at the hospital, before going home, to check on the injured firemen. He might as well get as much of the story as possible, and if the injuries were serious, he could stop at the newsroom and leave a short follow story.

An older and more experienced reporter might not have devoted so much attention and effort to the story, but Kindrake Smith was less than a couple of months out of journalism school and was on his first job. It also was one of his first important stories.

No fireman was seriously injured, so Smith had settled down for a chat with Dr. Jimson, who was not particularly busy at the moment. The doctor was telling the reporter about an emergency case the previous night when a sheriff's patrol car swept into the driveway and stopped at Emergency.

Two deputies brought in a woman. Smith judged that she was in her early thirties and possibly a very good-looking blonde under some circumstances.

In her present condition she immediately interested him for other reasons. Obviously she had suffered some sort of an attack. She wore a torn black silk dressing robe that looked too large for her—as if it belonged to a man—and there was an embroideried "V" on the robe.

After the routine of admitting her, and talk between the admitting attendant and the deputies, the woman was taken into an emergency treatment room where Dr. Jimson awaited her. The deputies remained behind in the reception room.

Smith went over to them and introduced himself, showing his press card.

"What's that all about?" he asked.

"Gang rape," one of the deputies said shortly. "A carload of punks."

'What happened?"

The deputy looked at the other as if questioning if they should give details to the reporter.

"It'll be a matter of record," Smith reminded them placatingly. He deliberately looked at the admittance card the attendant had just finished typing. "Married. Sarah Emmlin; husband Webster Emmlin"—followed by an address. Good part of town, he mused. The attendant frowned and snatched the card away from him.

"What's the full story?" Smith asked the deputies.

The talkative deputy shrugged a little and quickly told what they had learned; about the farmer's call; Sarah's story about being picked up and taken to the back road.

"Picked up where?" Smith asked.

"She didn't know."

"Didn't know?"

"Some of her story is confused." The deputy was young. He had earned his way through a local college on a football scholarship. He liked his job and he was ambitious. Maybe a newspaper friend would be helpful sometime. "We don't have all the answers yet."

"How about that robe? You don't spell Emmlin with a "V"."

"She didn't want to talk about that."

"Where had she been?"

"No answer there either."

"Well—thanks. Nothing else, huh?"

The deputy hesitated again and glanced at his older companion. The older deputy looked on noncommittally. The young deputy said, "Well, there's one other thing."

"By the way, what's your name?" Smith interrupted with a friendly smile.

"Collinger. Mike Collinger. My partner is Jack Tcharek."

"T-c-h-a-r-e-k," the older deputy spelled, almost automatically.

Smith jotted down the names.

"Don't use our names unless it's cleared," Tcharek said.

"Course not," Smith nodded. He looked back at Collinger. "What else doesn't add up about her?"

"Well, besides being raped, someone gave her one hell of a whipping. We asked her if the punks did that and she said 'No.' We asked who did, and she clammed up. Wouldn't talk any more about it."

Smith's eyebrows went up. He remembered his abnormal psychology.

"You mean it looks like a sadist case?"

Collinger shrugged. "You see a lot these days. You know how it is. It wouldn't be the first time."

"But the punks didn't do it?" Smith asked.

"According to her, she must have got the whipping someplace else. That gal was having a busy night."

"She doesn't look like a chippy," Smith said thoughtfully. "Emmlin—I wonder." He looked at a row of books on a general-purpose desk behind the admittance counter. He nodded and said to the attendant: "May I have a look at that city directory?"

The attendant—a tall, scowling woman in a white uniform—looked annoyed but gave him the book. Smith thumbed through the pages rapidly. He checked names and addresses and made a few notes on a folded piece of copy paper.

"Her husband works for an ad agency," he said. "This dame is no tramp out of a beer tavern. The part of town they live in—Emmlin's job—even that robe with the 'V'—say! I wonder what gives here?"

The two deputies glanced at the city directory and then at the reporter.

"Is she going to press charges?" Smith asked.

"I doubt it," Tcharek said. "A woman like that seldom will. Not when she's been ganged."

The door to the treatment room was opened and Dr. Jimson came out. His thin, gangling body looked awkward in his white coat. He blinked at the reporter and deputies through gold-rimmed eyeglasses that looked a little old for his thirty-odd years of age.

"Okay, Doc?" Tcharek asked.

"She'll be all right. Give her a little while. I'll give her a sedative and you can take her home. A nurse is helping her clean up now."

The deputies nodded and went over to sit in waiting chairs. Tcharek glanced around and lit a cigarette. Smith subtly herded the doctor across the room.

"What happened to her?" he asked.

The doctor found a crumpled, half-empty pack of cigarettes in a pocket of his white coat. He lit one.

"Ought to quit these," he said, and inhaled deeply. He looked at the reporter. "What happened to her? A gang of punks raped her. No tears or serious damage, but she's in some slight shock and she's going to be damned stiff and sore for a few days. They ought to horsewhip that gang of punks—if they could find them."

"I agree. But tell me, Doc—the deputies say she evidently was whipped. She said the punks didn't do that. What do you think?"

Dr. Jimson looked at him with a guarded expression in his eyes. He looked away and at the tip of his cigarette as if he were studying the coal with infinite interest. "So they told you about that?" he said.

"Yes. What about it?"

The doctor looked up again and squarely into Smith's eyes. "Look, Smith—why don't you skip it? The woman is a nice woman—I mean, she's from a good family—"

"I know where she's from," Smith said. He smiled thinly— a young, alert-appearing, fairly good-looking man wearing a smartly cut sports jacket, buttoned-down soft collar, knit tie and contrasting slacks. Some people thought his eyes were just a trifle too cold, his mouth a trifle too thin, his attitude a trifle too aggressive.

"Then you know that this isn't for your paper," the doctor said.

"Why not?" Smith asked. "She's Sarah Emmlin. Her husband is Web Emmlin. He works for an ad agency—an account executive. They live in a good part of town. They probably run with a set that makes our society pages occasionally. This excuses her from being news when she's been raped by a gang of delinquents and whipped by a sadist?"

"I didn't say she'd been whipped by a sadist."

"No, you didn't. But—off the record now—was she?"

The doctor considered his answer and the cigarette tip for a few seconds before he answered. "It looks that way." he admitted.

"She slipped and told the deputies that the punks didn't do that part of it."

"Possibly not," the doctor nodded. "There are some bruises beginning to show—counting time and all the rest, I'd say there might be a time element involved."

"Did she say if she is going to bring charges?"

"She said she wanted to be taken home—and I guess if anything more comes of it all, it will have to come out of the sheriff's office."

"Did she say if she could identify any of the punks?"

"She said she couldn't."

"Then that's it, I guess. Except for one thing."

"What's that?" the doctor asked.

"The city editor has been looking for everything he can find on these cases involving the young punks running loose around here. The city's in trouble with some of these gangs. He may want to make a story of it."

"Will he tread lightly? I mean about names?"

"Possibly. But in these rape cases we can make a lot of impact by telling the story—even if we don't identify the women or girls. In this case, the wife of a well-known businessman ..."

"So what are you going to do about it?"

"Not go to bed. In a couple of hours the city editor will be up—he's an early riser. I'll call him and find out what *he* wants to do about it."

"Maybe you'd better take it easy, Smith. There may be more than meets the eye in this one."

"You mean that 'V' on the man's silk robe—and my guess is that the robe is all she was wearing, right?"

"Yes," Dr. Jimson said. "To both counts. Her name is Sarah Emmlin, and neither name begins with a 'V' and her husband's name is Web. And all she wore was the robe."

"She'd be a damned good-looking woman with a good sleep and some of the wear and tear cleaned up," Smith said. "Pretty and stacked."

The doctor's eyes met his, but he didn't comment. Smith smiled slightly.

"Those damned punks!" he said.

The nurse who led Sarah to a shower room down a short hallway from the treatment room was young, pretty and recently graduated from a school of nursing. This was her first night in Emergency. She also was a virgin, and slightly embarrassed to be suddenly alone with Sarah after the doctor had left them. What should she say? How should she act?

"I'm sorry, Mrs. Emmlin," she said. "It must have been terrible." She wondered what it would be like to be manhandled and raped by a gang of men. She shuddered at the thought. Also she wondered if they had whipped their victim with a belt after-wards—or before. When would men do that? *Why* would they do it? Because she resisted them? Or was it just pure sadism or mania?

"A good shower will help," she said. "But first perhaps you'd better—" She blushed. "I mean, here's the hose and nozzle and—well, I'll be back in a few moments—or just call if you need me." She fled, painfully conscious of her embarrassment.

Sarah stared at the door that the nurse had closed. She felt dazed and numb from what had happened to her. The doctor had prescribed pills as a sedation, had suggested a quick bath before she took them, and then she was to go home to bed. He had assured her that there was nothing seriously wrong physically. She would be sore. She would have pain. But there was no physical injury of consequence.

Those had been his exact words: "no physical injury of consequence." She remembered them now and shut her eyes as she shuddered and leaned against a wall. Tears squeezed from her eyes. She had wept during the night. She had sobbed, hysterically at times, but now she wept quietly and bitterly; not for the pain and physical abuse she had suffered, but for what she had lost, for the memories that she could never lose, and for all the tomorrows that would never be like the yesterdays of her life.

The farmer's wife had been kind and understanding. She had taken Sarah to a bathroom and had given her a wash cloth, and there was hot water.

The two deputies had been concerned and respectful. They had used a siren as they hurried her to the hospital after they had determined that she did not need an ambulance.

In the car they had covered her with a blanket. They had her ride in the back seat while both of them sat in the front seat. One of them had used a radio to give a report. It had all reminded her of television shows she had seen.

Only now she wasn't at home, watching a TV show, safe, secure, as a hero arrived in time to save a heroine, as the police sirened to the scene at the exact moment when they were needed.

But they had asked the same kind of questions. What had happened? Where? When? Who? Could she recognize the men? Had the men beaten her? The farmer's wife had mentioned the whip lashes. What about the lash marks? Where did she get them? These questions after the routine questions! Name? Address? Your husband's name?

Then in the hospital, the attendant asking some of the same questions again. Your name? Your address? Your husband's name?

Standing in the shower room she let the tears stream down her face. She wasn't certain what answers she had given. She wasn't certain of anything. She was sick. Her back smarted. Her breasts hurt. Her head ached. Her mouth was sore and her lips were cut. The doctor had treated her superficial injuries. He had examined her—the embarrassing, necessary examination of a doctor examining a woman who has been raped to determine the extent of damage.

"Nothing torn. You'll be all right. I suggest ..." A natural suggestion to fit the circumstances, the necessity for proper cleansing.

This is happening to me, she had thought. I am the woman raped. Men—several men—men I wouldn't recognize on the street if I saw them—men or boys or both. Taking me. Being intimate with me. Taking by force what I so jealously guarded and gave as a gift. I'm dirty now. I'm dirty, dirty, dirty. She had wept then, during the examination, as she wept now after the nurse had left her.

After a time she opened her eyes and wiped the tears from her face with the flats of her fingers. She took off the black robe and hung it up on a hook. She turned on the water and adjusted it. The water was hot and comforting upon her. The soap had a clean, antiseptic, hospital smell.

She lathered and rinsed, and began to lather again. Suddenly she remembered the other suggested cleansing. She stepped out of the shower and dried herself. She should have reversed the cleansing tasks, but it was so difficult to think. Things were confused. She still was sick and now there was the sour taste of the alcoholic aftermath. A hangover. She shuddered in utter revulsion.

Quickly she used the equipment the nurse had brought for her and she saw there was another dry towel, so she showered again, quickly, working the soap into a heavy lather at her groin in the subconscious desperate desire to cleanse herself completely of the night and its trauma.

She rinsed and dried again. The nurse knocked at the door as Sarah was getting into the robe.

"Are you all right, Mrs. Emmlin?"

"Yes, thank you." *Mrs. Emmlin. I am Mrs. Emmlin, Web's wife. I spoke the marriage vows and deliberately I have been unfaithful twice. I have been raped. I don't know how many men have had me. I am used. I am Mrs. Emmlin and I am now as used as a prostitute.*

She shuddered again in her revulsion and abruptly she was desperately sick. She vomited into a toilet bowl hard, retchingly, so that she became faint and thought she would lose consciousness. She got down on her knees.

The nurse heard her and came in and helped her. After moments the nausea passed and the nurse got her a glass of water to rinse out her mouth. In a little while Sarah felt better. She thanked the nurse.

"May I go home now?" she asked.

"The doctor said as soon as you felt up to it, Mrs. Emmlin. The pills will help you sleep, and you're to go right to bed. The deputies are waiting to take you home."

"I don't know the doctor's name ... I don't know what hospital I'm in," Sarah said.

"You're in City General Hospital. It's Dr. Jimson, and I'm Miss Crumbein."

"You've been very kind."

They walked back along the hallway and through the empty treatment room. Sarah smiled weakly at the two deputies who got to their feet when the two women came into the waiting room. At the end of the counter the doctor was talking to a young man in a sport jacket and slacks. The young man came toward Sarah. She didn't recognize him.

"Mrs. Emmlin," he said. "I'm Kindrake Smith of the *Ledger*. Would you tell me what happened tonight?"

His words brought a new fear that struck with blinding impact. She could vizualize headlines and possibly a picture. Everyone—the whole world—could know what had happened to her.

"No!" she cried. The vehemence of her own voice startled her. She stared at the young man. "Oh, no ... please!"

"I don't want to upset you, Mrs. Emmlin, and you can be certain that everyone at the *Ledger* sympathizes with you, but it is only if people like you will help that we can put a stop to things like this. For the sake of all women in the city—"

"No," Sarah said again. She looked with pleading eyes to the deputies.

"That's enough," the older deputy said to Smith.

The doctor spoke in a sharper voice. "Leave her alone, Smith. That's an order." He hastened to them and he took one of Sarah's hands reassuringly. "You go home and get to bed. The sedatives will help. Call me later, if you wish."

CHAPTER TEN

L ike a good many other morning newspapers, the *Ledger* ignored a true regard for morning or afternoon. Its publishing day actually began shortly after noon when its first edition hit the street stands in a "blue streak" edition designed to take the edge off the competing afternoon newspapers.

To obtain quick sales and impact for the edition the *Ledger* editorial policy demanded a startling banner headline. The morning and home editions would be well tamed and almost conservative at times, but the "blue streak" edition headlined crime, sensational divorces, anything that could legitimately make a news story as long as it lent itself to a startling headline to give newsboys something to shout on business corners, and to catch the eye of pedestrians.

The *Ledger* also regarded itself as a "reform" newspaper, devoting considerable type to crime, youthful delinquency, corrupt government and a somewhat shocked attitude about the condition of the city, state, nation and world.

It also frequently was critical of the contemporary city administration, police department and public morals in general. All these things made for a good circulation, and with TV, radio and other media—to say nothing of two competing newspapers—bidding for audience and resulting advertising, the policy was carefully pursued.

The *Ledger* city editor—Al Grom, fiftyish, hard-driving, circulation-conscious—listened to Kindrake Smith's story with increasing interest. This kid reporter might have something. Even if the names would have to be played down, and even if the woman didn't press charges, a story was here. Possibly the very fact that she wouldn't press charges could be part of the story. The need for women to report assaults and press charges so that enforcements officers would be in a better position to obtain convictions was a point to feature.

"I think you've got something, Smith," he said over a telephone. "Now listen: It's Sunday and we'll have a clear beat with the blue streak, even if it's a light run and mainly hits the stands and corners. We'll follow up in the home edition for the morning.

"Here's what I want: Chase down the farmer who found her. Get an interview with him and his wife. I'll have someone cover anything additional that may turn up at the sheriff's office. We'll try to talk with the woman's husband. See if you can get a lead on the 'V' on that robe. I've heard about a group of our so-called better citizens who are playing a bedroom game. Maybe we're on to something."

He gave a few additional instructions in his terse, blunt voice, and then he called the managing editor. Shortly afterwards he called the chief editorial writer for the *Ledger*. Policy had been decided.

The Sunday edition of the "blue streak" was distributed on schedule and the headlines caught the eyes of thousands in the city who stopped for sandwiches, refreshments, beer or Sunday dinners, who shopped at markets or stores that were open for the holiday trade, who drove aimlessly about the city, and who did the things people usually do on a summer Sunday afternoon. Trucks also carried the papers to coastal resorts and other vacation spots. The Sunday "blue streak" was the only newspaper edition that filled the time between Sunday morning and Monday morning. It was a fairly light run, but it was a well-read edition.

The banner headline across the top of the edition on this Sunday afternoon was brief and explicit: GANG ATTACKS WOMAN.

The story, after a subhead, was a trifle ambiguous, but also explicit. It read, in part:

> The wife of a local businessman was criminally attacked early this morning by a carload of unidentified youths. The attack took place near a lonely country road in the Hillcrest area.
>
> The woman, dazed, beaten, and clad only in a black silk man's robe bearing the monogram "V", was found shortly before dawn on Hillview road by James Hoolstead, a farmer, who took her to his home.
>
> Two deputies from the sheriff's office answered Hoolstead's call and took the woman to City General Hospital, where she received medical treatment before being taken to her home.
>
> The victim—whose name is not being revealed by the *Ledger* at this time—is reported to have refused to press charges against her unidentified assailants. When interviewed by a *Ledger* reporter she refused to discuss the case.
>
> No explanation was made about the mysterious black robe.
>
> The woman's husband refused to talk with reporters late this morning.
>
> Hoolstead reported that the woman told his wife, Alice, that five youths had forced her into a car and had driven her to the Hillcrest area where she had been raped by her assailants.

Lash marks, obviously the result of a sadistic whipping, were not explained, but the woman intimated in a statement to sheriff deputies, Mike Collinger and Jack Tcharek, that she had received the marks prior to her encounter with the youths.

The *Ledger* usually ran "hold-over" editorials from the morning editorial page, but on this Sunday a new lead editorial was substituted, and also slugged for the Monday morning edition. The lead paragraphs indicated the newspaper's interest in the case:

The shocking sexual attack upon the wife of a local business-man by a carload of youths is but one of a series of similar outrages that have taken place in this community over the last few months.

It is unfortunate—as has been the case in many previous attacks—that the woman involved in the case refuses to press charges or aid the sheriff's office in apprehending the assailants.

While we can well understand a respectable woman's hesitancy to reveal the atrocious abuse to which she has been subjected, it is only when women will offer such aid that enforcement officers can hope to apprehend and convict delinquents and criminals responsible for the attacks.

So, with little or no velvet in its glove, the *Ledger* was embarking upon another editoral crusade. The combination of news story and editoral indicated to knowledgeable readers that more would certainly follow and that the word had come from the editor's desk that they were to build up the story into a community issue—probably in an attack upon juvenile delinquency, the local law enforcement agencies and public morals in general.

Not a few of the readers were to detect the reference to the mysterious black robe, the reference to a "businessman's wife," and the hardly concealed intimation that something odd flavored the circumstances of this particular story, especially with the black robe and the lash marks. These all constituted elements of scandal.

No one would be much more conscious of this than Web Emmlin. Most advertising men of experience readily spot the inception and build-up of an idea, or movement, or force in media. Web was no exception and his brief morning experience with a *Ledger* reporter had resulted in a deeply disturbing apprehension. Once the newspaper began to probe into Sarah's activities of the night, the results could be disastrous.

That damned robe, he thought. *With the "V," all they have to do is find out that the party was at Vember's last night, and they'll tag that robe in a hurry.*

Thank God it was Sunday! He would need a few more hours to get straightened around with himself before he had to be at the agency.

He had warded off the reporter by simply refusing to talk about what had happened to Sarah. By then he had called their family doctor, who had given Sarah a stronger sedative, and she was sleeping.

Web sat now in the living room with a glass of bourbon and water in one hand and the newspaper in the other. He had just purchased it at a near-by candy store. He stared at the headline and read the story again. He wished now that he had questioned Sarah more closely, but she had needed sleep and rest so much that he couldn't make himself badger her for more.

He shook his head and swallowed more of his drink, remembering the morning; beginning with his awakening and realization that the door chime was sounding, and that he had the sour taste of a hangover in his mouth.

For a few seconds he had a bad time when he remembered Altha. He glanced at the other bed. Altha was not there. He looked around the room. Her clothing was gone. Evidently she had left.

The door chime sounded insistently. He got up and put on a robe and went to the door. He opened it and Sarah stood there. A man in uniform was at her elbow, smiling uncertainly. He introduced himself as "Deputy Sheriff Collinger." Sarah wore a blanket draped over her. Beneath it Web caught a glimpse of black silk and a monogram.

"I'm sorry," Sarah said. She looked as if she was ill.

Collinger spoke. "Mr. Emmlin, your wife has had some trouble. We've brought her home. She can tell you about it...." He hesitated, and appeared to be embarrassed as he glanced at Sarah. "Unless you'd like to have me explain, ma'am ..."

She gave him a tired, forced smile.

"No ... no, I'll tell him. You've been nice. I want to thank you. She took off the blanket and handed it to him.

The deputy nodded and looked uncertainly at Web. "Understand, sir—it wasn't her fault." His words sounded almost like a warning, Web thought.

"Thank you," Web said, not knowing for what he was thankful. He stepped back to let Sarah come in as he watched the deputy return to the prowl car. Another deputy was waiting in the car. Collinger got in and they drove away. Web closed the door. Sarah was a forlorn figure in an easy chair in the living room. He saw that she wore nothing under the torn robe.

"What happened?" he asked, his voice reflecting concern.

She looked up at him and the tired smile came again. She seemed to be appraising him, evaluating him, almost looking at him as if he were a stranger.

When she spoke, her words said the last thing in the world he expected to hear.

"Web … I guess I don't love you. I'm sorry." She hesitated and before he could speak, she added, 'If I did, I'd be worried about telling you, and I'd want you to hold me and comfort me. But I don't feel any of those things."

"What happened?" he demanded, deeply perplexed by her attitude and words.

"I was raped," she said. "I guess the common expression these days is 'gang-raped.' Five men—boys—whatever they were."

He stared at her, shock in his eyes. "My God—but how? What happened?"

"I was running away from your friend Vember."

"Running away? What …?"

"Did you know he's a sadist along with other things, Web?"

She stood and undraped the robe and let it drop to the floor. She turned so that he could see her naked back, the welts; the angry, ugly marks.

"Look," she said, facing away from him. "You can see that part, but not the real hurt. The other. You can't see *that*. No one can, but it's there. What's the saying, Web? 'The inhumanity of man to man'? Is that it? You're a man of words. Is that what you men say?"

She turned and faced him with bitterness in her eyes. "Let me revise it a little, Web. Let me rewrite it. Twelve hours ago I couldn't have written it, because I wouldn't have known. But I can now."

"Sarah, for God's sake—"

"Listen to the line I want to write; 'Man's inhumanity to *woman!*' Isn't that better? Look at me, Web. Beaten. Raped. And the hurt you can't see—the *memory.* The knowing that it *happened* to me." She smiled tightly. "You don't look at me as you once did, Web. You haven't for a long time—and it's worse now. You don't see me as a woman you want to love or to cherish. What you see now—think now—is a used woman. A naked, blond, battered, bruised and well-used woman."

She shut her eyes and stood tensely with closed fists, tears squeezing from between her eyelids, her mouth trembling to suppress sobs. He watched her not knowing what to do or say.

"I forgot," she finally said. "Has she gone? Can I use my bed?"

"Sarah—yes, of course—but for God's sake Sarah! Look—I'll call Dr. Tonseth."

"I've had a doctor," she said indifferently.

"You still need one." He stepped toward her, a hand extended, almost helplessly. "Is there something I can do?"

She wiped the tears from her face with her hands.

"No ... nothing now. Or ever, I guess. It wasn't very good anyhow, was it?" She turned and walked naked from the room toward a hallway. When he followed her to their bedroom, she was on the bed, face down, sobbing hysterically. The welts were plainly visible. Web saw them and the muscles in his jaw tightened and bulged.

"The son-of-a-bitch," he said aloud. "The dirty son-of-a-bitch."

He covered her and then called their family doctor.

All that had happened several hours ago; before the reporter had come, and before he bought the newspaper.

He finished the drink and went to look in on Sarah. She still slept, heavily and in drugged relaxation. The doctor had told him she was not seriously injured. He had been shocked by the story of the rape, and Web had let him assume that the lash marks had come from the assault.

Even as he looked at Sarah, the muted telephone by the bed rang. He quickly lifted the receiver and answered the call.

Len Vember said, "Web? I just saw that story in the *Ledger*."

"I've read it," Web said tightly, trying to collect his thoughts, and to analyze his exact feeling about Len Vember.

"She was wearing my robe," Len said. "I don't know what happened to her. She—"

"You bastard!" Web said, surprised by his sudden anger. It was the first time in his life he had ever spoken harshly to a client. He wasn't even certain if he did love Sarah, or if he was outraged because he found the whole thing so revolting.

"Take it easy, Web," Vember said, harshly. "You're sure you didn't talk to the cops or to the newspaper about that robe? Or where you and Sarah were last night?"

"I didn't say, but they'll find out."

"Not if we keep the lid on."

"I don't know yet what *I'm* going to do."

"I'll tell you, Web. Nothing. Not if you want to keep the Vember account—and your job. You start trouble about this, and I'll make it so tough for you you'll wish to God you'd never heard of me."

"Don't threaten me," Web said. He tried to sustain his anger, but he was worried. If he lost the account he would probably lose his job. Vember could make it that tough for him.

Neither spoke for a few seconds and then Vember said in a slightly softer voice: "Web—I'm sorry this happened. Sorry for Sarah. We all had too much to drink. I probably got a little out of hand, but I wouldn't actually have hurt her. But this rape thing—Web, that's terrible. I mean it."

Web didn't answer. He didn't know what to say. He waited and Vember spoke again.

"Try to keep a clamp on the papers until we can figure this out, Web. Remember that others are involved. If a scandal about key game parties gets out, a lot of people are going to be hurt. *Really* hurt."

"I'm not looking for publicity," Web said curtly. "Don't worry."

"Okay. We'll talk about it tomorrow."

"All right." Web automatically waited until he heard the telephone line click dead. He replaced the instrument and looked at his wife again. She still slept. He supposed Vember wouldn't actually have hurt her too severely. He hated a sadist, but he could understand how it could happen. After all, a broad belt was nothing like a fine whip or the really dangerous—

He shuddered at his thoughts. "You can't excuse Vember," he told himself. "Nor rationalize his behavior. What in hell is wrong with me! As if I would even *think* about overlooking Len Vember's part in what's happened!"

After a moment he left the room and went to the front of the house, where he quietly dialed a number. Agnes Aiten answered the telephone.

"I have to see you," he said.

"What's wrong? You sound frightened."

Quickly he told her about Sarah. There was a long pause when he finished. Neither spoke, but he knew that Agnes still was at the other end of the line because he could hear her breathing.

"Well?" he finally said.

"I don't know, Web. What a terrible thing to happen to her. It makes me feel sick. I'm not certain I want to see you."

"But—I *have* to talk with you."

"You should stay there with her. Don't you want to, Web? She *is* your wife."

"And you know how it is with you and me."

"But she *needs* you now, Web. Love hasn't anything to do with it. She's another human being—"

"Oh, for God's sake, knock it off, Ag. I've got to see you and talk with you. Len Vember is involved. There may be hell to pay and I want us to know where we are before it starts. I don't want you involved if the lid blows off—and it damned well can."

"What do you mean?"

"Get a copy of the *Ledger*. The blue streak for this afternoon. And I'll be over in fifteen minutes. Sarah is under sedation. She'll sleep for another three or four hours, at least."

"All right. But only for a little while. I don't like any of this, Web. Not any of it."

"Save your opinions until you know the score," he said briefly.

"Sometimes, Web ... sometimes you're a bastard." She hung up.

"Sometimes I probably am," he said aloud.

CHAPTER ELEVEN

Carl Trojan heard about Sarah's ordeal shortly after arriving at work Monday morning. He and Lillian had driven to the coast to attend a family party staged by some of Lillian's relatives. They had arrived home late Sunday night, had gone to bed immediately, and were late in arising. They had not seen a copy of the "blue streak" at the beach, and Carl did not look at a newspaper until he arrived at his office.

The lurid headline of the attacked woman caught his attention. When he read the portion of the story dealing with the black, silk robe and the monogram, a small, cold knot seemed to tie itself in the pit of his stomach.

The black, silk and the V could very well be Vember. Sarah had indicated that she intended to stay for the key game and he had been angry and disturbed about it all Sunday. He wanted her. He wanted a divorce from Lillian and he wanted to marry Sarah. It was as simple as that. A basic equation.

The fact that the "V" was involved might mean Vember's robe, but there was nothing to indicate that the woman was Sarah. If she had played the key game, it did not necessarily follow that she would be with Vember, or that she would be wearing his robe. It could be any one of the other women who sometimes participated in the bedroom games.

But a premonition told him that it was Sarah. Finally, after several impatient cigarettes, he closed the door to his office and called Sarah. It was shortly after 10 A.M. She answered the phone.

"Are you all right?" he asked.

"Oh … Carl!" Her voice sounded a trifle startled, as if she were surprised to hear from him.

"I suppose it's crazy," he said, "but I've been reading the story in the *Ledger* about the woman who was attacked—and the black, silk robe with the 'V' monogram. I'm certain I'm wrong. Something like this couldn't happen to you. I just wanted to talk with you, and—"

"You weren't wrong, Carl," she said quietly. "The robe was Vember's. I was the woman."

"Sarah! My God! Not *you*—"

"Why not me, Carl?" she asked in a brittle voice. "Am I any different to Vember or to five men and boys in a car? I'm a woman. I have all the necessary equipment for their pleasure. I'm not different."

"Don't talk that way," he snapped. "Stop it. You couldn't help what happened. Listen, Sarah—I must see you. At once."

"Why, Carl? Everything is changed now."

"Not what I feel toward you."

"That's hard to believe."

He took a deep breath and spoke slowly and firmly. "What happened to you was a terrible thing—but not your fault. You can't let yourself be scared by it. Nor anything that led to it. One thing is important. I've made up my mind about us. I'm going to ask Lillian for a divorce. I want you to divorce Web. We can leave here. I've had an offer in South America."

Sarah listened to Carl's voice, the words he said and the thoughts he expressed. Somehow Carl had not been much in her thoughts during the last few conscious hours she had gone through; certainly not after the carload of youths had picked her up. But now she saw him again as someone in her life, and she remembered the afternoon at the cabin when it had begun.

For a short time Carl had been very important to her. She had wondered what it would be like to be his wife. She had thought about leaving Web for Carl.

Then the thing about Carl suddenly had seemed less important. Breaking up what was between Web and her, the unsuccessful marriage, had become more important. She had to find herself, and her voluntary decision to play the key game had been largely inspired by the perverse desire to experience what she could, destroy something, find something new, change her own image while there was still time.

Abruptly she realized that Carl had a right to know how she felt about him—at least, he had the right of the first infidelity and possession, for whatever it was worth. Furthermore, he was seriously considering a breaking up of his own marriage, and changing his way of life for her. She wasn't sure if she wanted him to take any irrevocable steps as yet.

"Don't, Carl. Don't do anything yet. We have to talk. I'm sick today. Couldn't we tomorrow?"

"If you'd rather, Sarah. But if you change your mind—"

"If I do I'll call."

"One other thing, darling. In that news story—the whip marks. Vember?"

She hesitated a second and then answered, "Yes."

"I ought to kill him," Carl said evenly.

"Don't talk that way, Carl. It won't do any good. Some of it probably is my fault. I played the key game—and if you can't accept *that* at face value, there's no purpose in our talking."

"I don't understand you," he said. "But I'm not worried about it. When we're married it'll be different."

"I shouldn't think you'd want me now."

"I do."

"Carl ... don't do anything rash. I mean—"

"I won't," he said. "Call me if you want to see me sooner."

"Carl—"

"Later," he said. She heard the click as he broke the connection.

A moment later, and before she could co-ordinate her thoughts about the conversation, the telephone rang again. She answered and heard Maxine Vember's voice.

"Darling ... I'm so *sorry!*" Maxine Vember said. "What a horrible thing to have happen!"

"Thank you, Maxine." Sarah tried to sound appreciative, but found it difficult and suddenly she realized that she intensely disliked Maxine Vember. She disliked both the Vembers. How had she ever got mixed up in such a horrible thing? It was beginning to be a nightmare.

"And don't think I'm excusing Len!" Maxine said sharply. "He shouldn't have done that to you. He's to blame for all this."

"I don't know," Sarah said wearily. "Maybe we get what we deserve."

"Don't be silly, darling. If he hasn't—well, I'm not going to talk about it. Not about Len. I know him. Remember, I'm married to him. Do you want to tell me about the other? What happened out by that road?"

"Why?" Sarah asked curtly. She couldn't conceal the dislike any further. Maxine was prying, seeking details.

"Well ... sometimes a woman wants to tell another woman about some things. A man can't understand. Only *women* really understand women."

"I'd rather not talk about it, Maxine."

"Certainly. Don't misunderstand me, darling. I'm just concerned and want to help. And after what Len did—I'm not certain what *I'm* going to do."

"That's *your* problem," Sarah said, suddenly too tired to conceal her dislike of the other woman.

"You're so right, darling. I won't keep you. I know you must feel terrible. Sore and everything. It must be a nightmare to have *five* men, one right after the other, and—"

"I'm sorry, Maxine. I have to hang up. Someone's at the door." She concocted the trite lie because she could think of nothing else. No one was at the door, and she hoped no one would be there all day. "I'll talk with you later, Maxine … good-by." She hung up.

While Maxine was talking with Sarah Emmlin, Web Emmlin was sitting nervously in Tad Lanner's private office in the agency. George Jorsen, the other principal in the firm, was with them. Both Lanner and Jorsen looked the part of account executives. They had formed and maintained a fairly good ad agency. They saw and thought alike on agency policy, on campaigns for their clients and on their theory of advertising.

They frowned as they regarded Web and Tad Lanner said, "A little while ago I had a very disturbing phone call from Len Vember."

"Vember?" Web echoed, feigning surprise. *So it's begun,* he thought. "I hope there's nothing wrong. There shouldn't be."

"Shouldn't there?" Jorsen asked in a matter-of-fact voice that belied the frankles skeptical look in his eyes.

"What did Vember say?" Web asked. He had no illusions about the reason behind Vember's call. This was the warning. Vember wanted silence. If Web played it right, everything would be fine between the agency and Vember. If he didn't, there would be trouble that could mean Web's job. The Vember account was Web's main insurance of a job, and Vember knew it.

For a moment he was tempted to resist Vember's warnings. He could offer to get off the account, to leave the agency. He could tell them that working with Vember wasn't worth it. Only jobs were difficult to find. He recognized his own capabilities and knew that too many men in the business far outshone him. He would have trouble finding nearly as good as the position he had attained with the agency.

The two agency heads had taken a few seconds to light cigarettes. Neither had answered his question, and he asked it again.

"What did Vember say?"

"That he was a little unhappy with the advertising. That he'd even called Alexis in to give him a presentation—which impressed him, he said."

"I don't understand that," Web said. "He told me last week that the last campaign had been getting results."

Lanner shrugged. "Don't misunderstand us, Web. We're not accusing you of anything, nor do we take much stock in what Vember thinks about the job we do for him. It's a good job. You're a good man on the account. It's just that—"

Jorsen interrupted. "We're simply wondering about the relationship between you and your wife and the Vembers, Web. We're not stupid. We know some of the things going on. Hell, Web—we've been at Vember's parties and know about the key game. And that story in the *Ledger*—the monogram on the black robe. It—well, it simply adds up."

"To what?" Web asked coldly, not liking the conversation.

"Frankly, we'd like to know if Sarah is the woman involved," Jorsen said. "If she is, it makes a difference in how we regard Vember's complaint and the phone call. If he's putting pressure on you—"

"All right. That's it. I don't expect we can keep it quiet—not from our crowd. So now you know, and what shall I do about it? Is his threat valid? If we lose the account, am I out of a job?"

Lanner and Jorsen flicked a glance at one another and Lanner picked up the conversation.

"Web, you know how we feel about you. You've been with us a long time. You're one of us—hell, it's a family here. Only—well, losing Vember's billing right now would hurt us. Considerably, I guess."

"And I haven't any other accounts of importance."

"You'd probably pick up some," Lanner said, making small, affirmative gestures with one hand. "We won't worry until it happens."

Web shook his head. "Let's not kid each other. There aren't any good accounts here that *I* could get. If there were, I'd have had them a long time ago. And I'm realistic. I'd be wise if I played along with Vember. That it?"

"You put us on a hell of a spot," Lanner protested. "Considering Sarah's part in this. And you know how we feel about her. But damn it, Web, the agency isn't a person. The agency is an impersonal thing, an entity in itself, a business. We can make it live or we can let it die—or kill it. If we let it die, a lot of people here are out of work. It's their livelihood."

"Knock off the speech," Web said, almost angrily. "You don't have to make it. I know that you need Vember's billing to keep going right now. And you're right. I can't make you lose an account because I'm sore as hell at Vember."

"There isn't any room for personalities in business—not if the business *depends* upon there being no room for personalities."

"Now, Web, don't think that we—" Jorsen began to speak, placatingly, but obviously relieved.

"I know what you think," Web said. "So for Christ's sake shall we drop it? I'll assure Vember that I'm not going to jeopardize his goddamn lousy soul by talking out of turn or telling all. But I can't stop them from snooping—and someone eventually may put two and two together, and I can't help that. However,

I'll respect the agency and not try to wreck it deliberately. Is that what you want me to say?"

Lanner was watching him with unsmiling eyes and a slight tightness of lips. "That's about it, Web," he said. "It's unpleasant to lay it on the line this way, but that's it. It's not just you, or George here, or me. We need that billing right now. If we lose it, about five others outside that door may be hunting jobs within a couple months."

"Okay," Web said. "Okay."

"We'll see how things go," Lanner said carefully. "I hope it works out. I think it will. If it doesn't—and it's a choice of you or Vember ..." He shrugged.

"You need the billing," Web said evenly.

Lanner nodded. "We need the billing. And unfortunately, we have a feeling that if you do what Vember wants you. to do—keep your mouth shut, and Sarah doesn't upset things—everything will be fine. And that if we don't treat you nice under those circumstances Vember might make it a little rough all around."

"That's plain enough," Web said.

"One other thing," Jorsen said. "We're not prudes, Web. We've been around. But we don't like scandal. We don't like our people mixed up in it. Scandal is bad for business. Clear?"

"Like you said—it's a business," Web nodded. "Anything else?"

"No. But maybe you'd better call Vember and smooth things over."

"I'll do that," Web said curtly.

"Fine," Jorsen nodded. He exchanged another glance with his partner. "Anything else to contribute to this?"

"Hell, no! Just glad it's over and ironed out—at least for now. Knew Web would see how it is. A business."

"I'll call Vember," Web reiterated without comment upon Lanner's words. He turned to leave and Lanner stopped him again.

"Web ..."

Web turned.

"You and Aggie," Lanner smiled good-naturedly. "I know there's nothing there. Just working together. But you know how people are. There's been a little talk. Understand?

Strangely, Lanner's words were more disturbing than the previous conversation had been. He didn't want anything upsetting his relationship with Agnes. Not right now.

"Nothing to it," he said, forcing a smile. "Don't worry about that. I mean it."

"Sure," Lanner smiled. "That's what I told George."

Web lit a cigarette. "That's all?" he asked.

Jorsen nodded. "Nothing personal, Web."

"Of course not," Web smiled grimly. "It's a business—that's all. Just a business."

He left the office and gently closed the door after him.

CHAPTER TWELVE

Len Vember picked up a copy of the Monday "blue streak" edition on the way back to the dealership after lunch. Quickly he scanned the front page. There was a rehash of the morning story, with nothing of consequence added, other than a statement from the sheriff that his force was attempting to patrol the county roads and highways as completely as possible. He was aware that other assault cases had been reported. He knew that incidents involving youths, mostly from the city, were not uncommon. He was doing all that he could.

There was evidence that the *Ledger* intended to keep the fire burning. A corner box on the front page read:

STARTING TOMORROW—
A SPECIAL REPORT ON CRIME IN DOUGLAS CITY.

Len read the paper again in the privacy of his office and sighed in relief. Evidently his crack-down on Web was having effect. Unless Sarah brought charges so that the whole thing became a police matter, there wasn't much that the newspapers could do.

He lit a cigarette and after a moment he opened a cabinet door and took out a bottle of bourbon. He poured himself a quick, stiff drink and put the whiskey away.

He hadn't intended to use the leather belt on Sarah. He hadn't done anything like that since the last time in Los Angeles when he'd had the urge and had found a willing prostitute.

His tendency toward sadism was the one thing that Maxine would not tolerate. She was firm about it.

"I've done a lot of things, Len," she told him the first time he had experimented with slapping her during the height of a passionate hour. "But I don't like that. Never do it again. I won't take it from you or any man. I never have and I never will. Is that clear?"

Her sharp reprimand had killed the passion that gorged him at the moment. He was always to remember how quickly she had changed from an abandoned, demanding woman to the angry, cold woman who spoke the words in sharp, concise sentences. There was no mistaking her meaning.

"All right," he had smiled. "No more."

As suddenly as she had flared in anger she had reverted to the available, desiring woman. She even had smiled and had run a hand along the side of his face, in an understanding gesture.

"I know how it can be with a man sometimes," she had said. "Some of the girls used to go for it. The pay was good. And we all know that some men can't help it. There are women just as bad. You know that, too. It's just that—well, it's not for me. Anything goes but that."

"I said all right."

"If you have to have that sometimes, I won't mind if you find a girl. Some of them actually like it. And I don't think you'd hurt any girl very much. Just enough for your own kicks."

"Okay—you talk too much."

He had pulled her to him again, and they had continued their love-making in a more controlled atmosphere. He never had attempted to exploit his streak of sadism with her again.

As a matter of fact, he was afraid of his trend toward the deviation. He realized that it could get him into trouble. It could be dangerous. So he had controlled it fairly well. Fortunately, it was not strong, and on those occasions when it flared to the surface, he usually managed to stifle it.

With Sarah things had been different. She excited him as few women did. He had not wanted to use the belt, but once the idea had crept into his mind, and as she responded with increasing fervor to his skillful attentions its use had become a compulsion that he could not resist.

Now, as he had always feared it might, his surrender to the compulsion was bringing him trouble. He felt easier since reading the latest edition of the newspaper, but he was far from being out of the woods yet.

"Never again," he smiled wryly.

His inter-office telephone sounded and he answered it. His secretary's voice was efficiently impersonal.

Mrs. Lancotte is here to see you. She says it's urgent."

He instantly pictured the Lancotte woman as he had seen her in the office not too long before—the brown eyes, the golden hair, the tanned skin and the smooth, rich lines of a well-formed woman as she undressed.

Vaguely he wondered why she had returned. Certainly another car payment was not yet due. Of course, there was always the possibility that a woman would return because she was compelled to return. At any rate—and despite the worry of the day—there was no sense in sending her away. Possibly a little distraction would ease the tension that had built within him.

"Send her in," he said.

He watched the door open and he smiled a welcome as she came in. She had changed the summer sheath for a skirt and blouse. She wore no hat, and she looked like a schoolgirl, home for the summer from the university, rather than a housewife who was addicted to horse racing and who didn't mind paying a car installment with the services of her body.

She closed the door after her and returned his smile as he walked across the room and sat at the desk. She carried a large, straw, all-purpose handbag that looked imported and smart.

"Hello, Len," she smiled. "I can call you Len, can't I? I mean after—"

"Certainly, Jenny."

"Then you *do* know my first name! You must have looked at the contract after I left."

"Jenny is a good name," he evaded.

She smiled contagiously. "At first you called me Mrs. Lancotte. Then—after we started—you called me 'baby'—and toward the end you called me a hot little bitch, remember?"

He laughed. He enjoyed this girl. "That's a compliment," he said. "Few women are."

"You said a good many other significant little things while it was going on," she said, still smiling and looking into his eyes, as if she were greatly amused. "You were quite complimentary about certain parts of my anatomy ... about my ability ... and other things."

"Why shouldn't I be?" he asked. "I don't remember exactly what I said—but that was because you're pretty much on the terrific side."

"Would you like to know what you said?" she asked quietly.

"Not especially. Maybe I'd just like to say them again."

Still smiling, the amused, knowing, impudent smile, she shook her head. "No, Mr. Vember. You've had it. But literally, I mean, you've had it. And you should know how you sound. Let me demonstrate."

He watched her as she took a small, neat case from her large handbag. Apprehension was building in him.

"This is a transistor tape recorder," she said. "It runs on batteries. It's very good, quite expensive, exceedingly efficient. It was in my handbag the last time I was here. I'll run some of the tape for you—and I might warn you that this is a copy of the original tape which Harold has safely hidden away. So it won't do any good to try to destroy it—nor our expensive equipment. Listen—"

She flipped a switch and Len heard her voice: *Mr. Vember, I simply can't raise the money.* He heard his reply and parts of the conversation, including his reference to her husband: "*We wouldn't want any trouble between you and your husband, Mrs. Lancotte.*"

The woman stopped the machine for a few seconds. "That identifies you and me and the situation," she smiled. "Now—here's the proposition. I got it from you so easily, Mr. Vember! But then, we'd checked on you after we heard a story or two from some of the girls. You've made a habit of taking out the payments 'in trade,' as the saying goes. Listen."

She snapped the switch. He heard his voice in the conversation that had led to the proposition: her plea that he use a contraceptive; his answer; her final acquiescence: *all right ... I'm ready to pay up—whenever you're ready to collect.*

Len felt anger rise like a sudden illness. He lit a cigarette with trembling fingers. The woman watched him with amusement. She had stopped the machine again.

"Now," she said. "Listen to how you sound ... what you say ... and a few other details."

He listened. There could be no mistaking what was happening. He realized how cleverly she had made him talk, say things that were obvious, almost clinical, and certainly incriminating.

"All right," he snapped. "Turn it off."

She flipped the switch, lit a cigarette and sat back in her chair.

"It's a nice job of recording for such a small machine," she said. "Don't you think so?"

"How much?" Len Vember asked.

"You're doing well in this dealership. We think twenty thousand dollars would be about right."

"Or else?"

"Copies of the complete tape, with a pertinent letter of explanation that will certainly bring auditions of the tape, will be sent to the vice-president in charge of sales for the car you handle. That may cost your franchise. A copy to your wife, of course. A copy to the Chamber of Commerce, the Better Business Bureau, the Chief of Police—" She smiled and quickly explained, "We'd be far gone by then, and Lancotte is not our name, and, after all, I don't mention blackmail in the *tape* so we'd be committing no serious crime. I'd just be a girl who laid you to pay an installment on a car."

"You must have really set this one up," he said angrily.

"And we'd also send a tape to the Douglas City ministerial association, the president of the PTA and—"

"You've made your point. But not twenty grand. Five at the most."

"If we don't want to take five?"

She stared at him impudently, her lips twisted in the amused smile, head up, breasts jutting out beneath the thin blouse. He looked at the golden-colored hair, the dark brown eyes, the tanned skin. A strange and ominous compulsion stirred within him.

"Who do you think you are?" he said in a low, taut voice. "Trying a blackmail deal like this on me? You chippy. You two-bit whore. You and your pimp!"

His anger was like a turbulent, rising, uncontrollable tidal wave. He felt muscles tense. Hotness coursed through him, even into his groin. He felt suddenly strong and dominant. Above all, he felt vengeful. There was a way to handle a thing like this! To punish! To crush!

The woman no longer smiled. She stared into a face that suddenly fascinated her by the naked, unreasonable anger it revealed. This was not what she had expected. She and Harold had pulled their game before, but never had a man acted like this. She was frightened.

"Look, Mr. Vember—don't try anything!—" The audacity was completely gone from her voice. She was almost plaintive. She stood and started to back away.

Len Vember got up and came around the desk. For a second he stood over her, glaring down into brown eyes that were wide in fear.

At that second Vember could not have analyzed his own thoughts or emotions. He was angrier than he could ever remember, yet the anger was mixed with something else.

He had a tremendous, violent desire to lay his hands on this woman—not only in anger, but also because she was a woman. He must beat her, subjugate her, dominate her, punish her. The male must dominate the female. The male must punish the female. The male must display his mastery over the subservient female!

He hit her. It was a hard, open-hand slap that sent her reeling across the room. He followed her, stalking, grasping her left wrist to hold her.

She screamed as he tore her blouse down the front. She screamed again as he hit her squarely in the mouth with the back of a hand.

Desperately she tried to escape and momentarily broke loose. She fell over a chair. The chair caught a stand lamp and sent it crashing across the desk, knocking the tape recorder to the floor.

Vember reached down, and jerked her upright. He tore more clothing from her and slapped her across the face repeatedly.

He had found words now. "Bitch! ... Chippy! ... Slut! ... Not *me*, you don't! You don't take *me!*"

She screamed again and again. The door to the outer office opened and the frightened face of Vember's secretary was there for an instant. The girl turned and ran out to the street, trying not to scream.

Several salesmen and customers in the display room stared at the back offices. The screams continued, punctuated by the sound of hard slaps. Two of the salesmen started toward Vember's office.

The street door was open and the secretary ran back into the building. Behind her a traffic cop, still clutching a book of traffic tags he had been using for overparked cars, followed her. She stopped at the door to Vember's office. The cop hurried past her, jamming the book of tags into a pocket.

Abruptly the slapping stopped. The woman's screams were replaced by the sound of hysterical sobbing. The salesmen slowed and walked uncertainly toward the office.

The traffic cop pushed Vember roughly through the doorway. The cop looked angry and when Vember tried to resist the shoving hand, he jerked Vember forward so sharply that Vember stumbled to his knees. The cop pulled him up and looked at a salesman.

"Where's a phone?" he snapped.

The salesman nodded toward a desk. The cop went to it.

"Dial nine first and then your number," the salesman said, staring past the cop at Vember with puzzled, unbelieving eyes.

The cop dialed the number and asked a desk sergeant to send help. He replaced the telephone and looked at the secretary.

"You'd better go in there," he suggested. "That woman needs some help."

Vember was breathing hard. He avoided the eyes of the small crowd that was collecting. Automatically he straightened his necktie and smoothed back his gray hair with the palms of his hands.

"All right, officer," he finally said. "I'm okay now. That little bitch tried to blackmail me. I lost my temper."

"You may have lost more than that, mister," the cop said. "Believe me."

An hour later a lieutenant of detectives, an assistant prosecuting attorney and several other officers listened to Jenny Lancotte tell a fairly convincing story. On the lieutenant's desk was the tape recorder.

Jenny Lancotte's face was swollen. Her mouth was cut and still oozed blood. A darkened area on one cheek suggested the beginning of discoloration. She was wearing an office smock that Vember's secretary had loaned her to replace the torn blouse.

"Again, Mrs. Lancotte," the detective said. "Mr. Williams from the district attorney's office would like to hear your story."

Carefully she repeated the story she had concocted for the police officers: of having spent her husband's money for horse racing, of going to the dealership to try to arrange to make car payments later, of the meeting with Len Vember, and the subsequent submission to him.

At this point her story varied—convincingly—from the truth:

"Then this morning he asked me to come in. He brought out this recorder from his desk and played the tape. He asked me if I'd like to have my husband hear the tape. I was frightened. He told me that he wouldn't give the tape to my husband if I would consent to do more things with him."

She stopped and wiped tears from her eyes. Her voice trembled a little as she continued.

"Hearing the tape seemed—well, it seemed to excite him. He asked me to take my clothes off and when I protested—he—he attacked me and started to hit me. I guess you know the rest—the policeman came and then you people found the recorder and tape."

The lieutenant said, "Vember insists that you tried to blackmail him."

"That's a lie," she protested. "Look what he did to me. He might have killed me!"

The lieutenant nodded. "You'll bring charges of assault against him?"

She hesitated and looked from one face to the other.

"Yes," she finally said. "I guess my husband will find out anyhow. I—I don't know what else to do. But I didn't try to blackmail him. He lies."

The lieutenant exchanged a look with the assistant prosecutor. The attorney nodded slightly.

"It's a good story, Mrs. Lancotte," the lieutenant said. "But not quite good enough. You'll have to explain something else."

"What?"

"Vember insisted that we dust that recorder for prints. We found plenty of yours—and some of a man, probably your husband's because they don't match Vember's. In fact, we found none of Vember's prints. It looks pretty much as if you brought the recorder to the office and played the tape. Why?"

Jenny Lancotte wiped tears from eyes that now were cold and thoughtful. She had dropped the pretense of fright and outrage.

"All right. So I brought the tape and played it for kicks. If he says I tried to blackmail him—"

"He does."

She bit at her lower lip. "I want to talk with my husband."

"Later. We picked him up about an hour ago. He has a record."

"Okay! So he has a record. Did you find out that I have one, too? Is that it? One of your prize citizens slapped me around, but because I've got a record you're going to let him get away with it?"

"You have quite a record for a girl who spent some time at a university, Jenny. You've worked as a prostitute. You managed to beat a shoplifting rap. The man you say is your husband is a narcotics user. Let me see your arm."

"Go to hell."

"Is that what started you? When you became a user?"

"Okay. So that's what started me, but I've kicked the habit. Are you going to railroad me?"

"Are you going to press charges against Vember?"

She was thoughtful and the coldness of her eyes gave the impression that she might have a good mind despite the background.

"Is he charging me with attempted blackmail?"

"That's his defense."

"Then I'll charge him with assault, attempted rape and everything in the book. Too many witnesses saw me after he finished with me to let him beat the rap. And you've no proof that I tried to blackmail him. The only proof you have is a tape that says I laid him to make a car payment—and that I got a taping of it and brought it back to play it over for kicks."

The lieutenant looked at the attorney and shrugged. The attorney nodded. "She has a case," he said. "She has the witnesses. His case—I don't know."

They took her from the office and in an outer room Kindrake Smith from the *Ledger* waited. As soon as they would see him he talked with the lieutenant and attorney.

"She's making a complaint against Vember," the lieutenant admitted. Smith pressed for more details.

A half-hour later he interviewed Jenny Lancotte. She seemed indifferent about answering his questions, neither evading nor amplifying.

Finally Smith said, "How did you happen to take the recorder there in the first place? What made you think that Vember would play ball with you?"

She allowed him the first smile she had displayed during the interview.

"My God, are you that naive?" she asked. "Any call girl in town could tell you about the games he plays. If he can't get some of his society friends to bed down with him, he calls in a girl. Mostly he doesn't have to—not between the girls he gets on the hook through car payments and the key game he and his wife play with their friends."

"Key game? What's that?"

She looked at him in disbelief and shook her head. "You *are* naïve," she said. She described the key game. She went on from there to tell what other girls had told her, the rumors, the reported nude swimming parties, some of the more prominent names that frequently were mentioned.

Smith listened attentively, taking notes, and prodding with a question now and then.

"And you're going to press charges against Vember?" he asked.

She looked at him and finally asked for a cigarette. He held a light for her and watched her inhale deeply.

"Mr. Smith," she said, "I don't know exactly what I'm going to do, or what he's going to do, or what the police and that young DA's assistant intend to do. But I do know that any charges against me for attempted blackmail aren't going to cause half the ripple that my charges against him will cause!"

"Your husband denies any knowledge of this," he said.

"He would," Jenny Lancotte said. "He's already a twotime loser."

A detective joined them. "The lieutenant wants to talk with you again, Mrs. Lancotte," he said.

She nodded and smiled again at Smith. "As my grandmother used to say, the fat's in the fire. So go ahead and print all of it. You can use my name—Jenny Lancotte. I don't mind. The folks back home won't recognize it as mine. And ... happy hunting, newspaperman!"

For Kindrake Smith and the *Ledger* it proved indeed to be a happy hunting ground. Paralleling the series of articles about the crime situation in Douglas City, the newspaper covered the "Lancotte-Vember" case in lurid detail. Other newspapers picked up the tempo in self-defense.

Scandal rocked Douglas City in severe, small jolts as Jenny Lancotte made her charges and as Vember admitted or tried to evade accusations.

Editorials questioned the morals of "some high-placed citizens" in the community. Pressure for quick judicial action, somewhat spurred by a desire of the city and county administrations to get out of the limelight, resulted in a prompt trial for Vember.

During the few intervening days of turmoil, the couples who had participated in Vember parties spent sleepless nights and nerve-racked days, fearing each morning to see their names in the *Ledger*, to have the glare of exposure thrown upon them.

Jenny Lancotte's reference to the possibility that Len Vember might own the mysterious black, silk robe with the letter "V" on it had released a flood of speculation, rumor and stories.

Telephones rang, voices spoke rapidly in gossiping, eager tones. It became expedient to have only a "casual acquaintance-ship" with Len Vember.

The fact that the Vembers had entertained the eventful Saturday night was adroitly mentioned in a *Ledger* story.

Then—unusually soon, it seemed—Len Vember was tried, convicted and sentenced. His blackmail charge against the Lancotte woman failed to hold up.

CHAPTER THIRTEEN

The morning after the trial Carl Trojan put down a copy of the *Ledger* and regarded his wife, Lillian, with serious eyes.

"She made the assault and attempted rape charge stick," he said evenly. "Vember drew a sentence. We knew that yesterday afternoon. But the rest of it is here. The Lancotte woman got the rumors about swimming parties in the nude into her testimony. She also said she'd heard rumors about the key game. She did a lot of talking and the *Ledger* picked it up. No names, of course, just rumors."

"I read the story before you came down," Lillian said. They were at the breakfast table and she poured another cup of coffee and thoughtfully sipped it. "You've skipped mentioning an important part."

"What?"

"What the Lancotte woman said about that rape case and about the robe with the 'V' monogram. Suggesting that the police might well investigate that in connection with Len Vember's activities."

Carl looked at her levelly. "That means something?"

"Certainly it does. We know that the woman in that rape case was Sarah Emmlin. Maybe the *Ledger* hasn't said it, but half the city knows it by now. That farmer described her, and when Maggie Parned and Maurine Gonther stopped in to see Sarah, one look at her settled it. They said she looked terrible. They've told everyone they've seen, too."

"Damned malicious gossips," Carl snapped.

"Did you think she looked bad?" Lillian asked calmly.

For a few seconds he appeared to be a trifle surprised, and then angry.

"What makes you think I've seen her?"

"Because Maggie called me and I decided to stop in and see Sarah myself. I drove over there, but your car was parked in front of the house."

"I saw her."

"I think you've seen a lot of her, Carl. I think you've been very upset about this whole thing."

He carefully stubbed out a cigarette he had just lighted. "Are you trying to say something, Lillian?"

"Yes. There's no use pretending that our marriage has been anything but a marriage in name only for quite a while. You don't love me, and I stopped loving you a long time ago, Carl. I just didn't want to play games with anyone else—no key game, no experimenting with adultery. Maybe I'm rather sexless. Maybe I never did care much for it. But I certainly don't now, and I'm certain you know that."

"It's been obvious for some time," he said bitterly. "This is all a prelude to something. Just what?"

"That you probably want a divorce. That you've probably been having an affair with Sarah. When you look at her, it shows. And this: I won't give you a divorce, Carl. So if you're getting noble ideas about taking Sarah out of it all—if you still want her after she's become so ... shall we say, shopworn?—just don't try the divorce. I like things the way they are. I don't want to change anything."

He stared at her with hard, brown eyes, his mouth tightened. When he spoke, he obviously was fighting to control his voice.

"*Why*, Lillian? If there's nothing left between us—*why?* What do you gain? What's in it for you?"

"I enjoy my life. I keep busy. You earn a good salary. You're a gentleman, despite your probable infidelity. I wouldn't want to be single again, and I certainly wouldn't want to marry anyone else. It wouldn't be worth the emotional trauma of making another man understand what I want and what I don't want."

"I could leave you. Just pick up and go."

"I doubt if Sarah would go with you. If you tried, I'd bring you back, Carl. You won't make a fool of me."

Carl carefully folded the newspaper and placed it on the table. He got up and looked down at his big-framed, athletic-looking, wife, noticing that the sun had dried her skin too much, that she was beginning to get a few wrinkles around her eyes, and that her chin was beginning to show a small fold of looseness.

"I won't make a fool of you, Lillian. No one could. You're too damned sure of yourself, too dominant and too overpowering in your own particular way. Even if people know that we run with the Vember crowd in occasion, no one will ever suspect you of being involved in nude swimming parties or the key game. And they'll be right. They'll also believe that I'm in the clear. You're that powerful with your—your 'image,' as the advertising people say. It would carry over to me."

"That's quite a speech for an engineer."

"Quite a speech, Lillian. I hope you remember it."

He left the table without looking back. A few moments later Lillian thoughtfully read the story again, beginning with the headline:

CAR DEALER
FOUND GUILTY

There was a courtroom picture of Len Vember and another of Jenny Lancotte. The *Ledger* called it "the sensational trial that has shocked the city with implications of widespread immorality touching a group of middle-aged couples in the community."

While Lillian was reading the story again, Maxine Vember parked her car a mile away in front of the Gateson home. She glanced up the driveway to make certain that Tom Gateson's car was gone from the double garage. The open door revealed only Altha's small foreign car.

She went to the door and touched a doorbell. In a few moments Altha opened the door. Her eyes looked red as if she had been weeping.

"Oh—Maxine! I didn't expect to see you!"

She appeared to be flustered as she opened the door for her guest.

In the house Maxine turned toward Altha. She put her hands on Altha's shoulders and pulled her close and kissed her on the cheek.

"Darling!" she said. "What's wrong?"

"Tom and I quarreled. I guess I'm just upset about every-thing—and since that night it's been so *different.*"

"Since you and I found one another?" Maxine asked softly.

Altha shook her head, as if she were confused and didn't know the proper answers.

"Is there some coffee left?" Maxine asked cheerfully.

"Yes ... I guess so."

"We'll have some, and a good talk."

Maxine put her arm around Altha's waist and led the way to the kitchen. She insisted that her hostess sit down at the table while she poured the coffee. Then she sat at the table and lit a cigarette.

"There! Now we can talk."

"Maxine, I don't know what—"

"Let me, darling," Maxine interrupted. "First—about Len. The paper didn't have all of it. He'll have to serve a sentence, but our attorney assures us that the judge will recommend psychiatric treatment. That's really the trouble, Altha. But you must know that. Especially since the thing with Sarah."

"But aren't you—I mean—"

"Disturbed? Not particularly. I might have been before Saturday night, but not now. I think I'll divorce him, Altha. I know what I want now. I found it Saturday night—with you."

"But Maxine! I don't—"

"I know, my love—you're all upset about this business between you and Tom, and all of the things between you and me happening so suddenly, and you'd never had experience like that before. But it's going to be wonderful. You should leave Tom. You know that, Altha. We could get an apartment together and—"

"Stop it! Stop talking this way, Maxine. It isn't like this. I don't feel this way."

"You don't love Tom," Maxine said calmly. "You know that. You hate the sex part with him, and everything about living with him. You know that. You've as much as admitted it—"

"Maxine ... *please?*" Altha was weeping again. "Please leave me alone? I'm so confused and—I can't do what you're suggesting. Please? ... Won't you leave me alone? I don't want to be that way. Don't you understand? *I don't want to be that way—a lesbian!*" She was sobbing now, almost hysterically.

Maxine put a hand out and gently touched Altha's cheek.

"I know, darling … it's hard to believe it's happening to you at first, but soon you'll accept it and be happy. I'll make you very happy. As I did Saturday night—and you remember that, darling."

"I don't want to remember," Altha sobbed.

"But you will," Maxine said gently. She stood. "I have to go now. I'm going to talk to our lawyer about divorce. I think this trouble Len is in will probably be enough grounds. And I'll see you later—and when we get our apartment—"

"Maxine, I'm not! Please—I'm *not!*"

Maxine smiled and bent over and kissed Altha on the forehead.

"It will be all right," she said. "I'll take care of everything."

She left by the back door, smiling confidently as she went to her car.

For a long time after Maxine had left, Altha sat at the table. Her quarrel with Tom had been bitter and Tom had as much as asked for a divorce.

The night before she had received a telephone call from her parents. The implications of the Vember crowd's immorality had shocked them. They questioned her sharply about the frequency with which she and Tom had gone to the Vember parties, and finally about the nude bathing suits and the key game.

"I don't know anything about them," she had lied desperately. "It's all malicious gossip. Rumors." She had managed to convince them, but she had hung up feeling almost ill in her disgust. She remembered the previous Saturday night and all that it had brought.

Her parents would never understand. Probably no one in the city would really ever understand once the stories began to circulate, and the scandal began to break over the heads of the group.

Probably the only person who would understand would be her aunt in New York who worked on a national magazine. Her Aunt Liz who had been married twice and divorced twice and who had carved out a career for herself in the East. They corresponded frequently and Altha always had been the favorite niece.

The thought of her aunt seemed to inspire clearer thinking. After a time she poured more coffee and her weeping stopped.

She felt a sense of urgency. She had to get away from Tom because her marriage was a failure. More poignantly, she had to get away from Maxine Vember because she desired so deeply to be with Maxine.

"I will not!" she said aloud again. "I will *not* be a lesbian!"

Impulsively she called her mother. At first it was difficult to talk about Tom and the marriage that was breaking up, but it seemed that her mother had suspected trouble. Furthermore, she seemed to have the impression that Tom had tried to entice her daughter into the "wildness of that Vember crowd."

"I've made up my mind, Mother," Altha said. "I'm going to leave Tom. At least for a—a sort of cooling-off period. Do you think Aunt Liz would take me in for a while?"

"She'd love to! And I'll give you money to go."

"Right away, Mother!"

"At once. Maybe your father wouldn't object to my flying back with you. He's been worried about you, too. This will come as no surprise to him."

"Maybe if I went alone ... I mean, Mother, I need to be alone and think. Maybe later you could come back. But right now I'd have a place to stay there and Aunt Liz is gone so much of the time."

"Of course, dear. But you start packing right now. I'll come over and help. You probably can get a plane out this afternoon!"

"All right, Mother. And—and I think I'll just leave a note for Tom. I—I don't want another scene."

"Of course not. I'll be right over."

Altha hung up and lit a cigarette.

"I won't even say good-by to Maxine," she whispered. "I'd be afraid to—I might not go...."

Tom Gateson stalked into his office that morning without greeting any of his fellow employees. The quarrel with Altha had left him in a vile humor. On top of everything else, this mess about Vember had him on edge. He was very conscious of his family's position in the community. He feared his father's wrath, if the older man learned about his son's association with the Vembers.

His Saturday night experience with Maxine had been unnerving. He knew that he had failed again, and now he was not certain that he would not fail every time. He had belatedly approached Altha to get a definite physical answer to his problem. If he could be fully potent again with her, he would know at least that he was still capable of being a man.

Altha had repulsed him. Since that Saturday night she had been like a different person. When he had awakened late that Sunday morning, Altha was home and up. She was oddly uncommunicative about her activities of the night before—simply saying that it hadn't worked out well, that she had come home early, that she had slept in the guest room. No, she didn't know when Maxine had left.

From that morning on, through the immediately following days of tension and apprehension about the Vember mess, and the news about Sarah Emmlin, they had quarreled frequently and about everything, or anything.

This morning had been another senseless episode, starting over something already forgotten, but ending in bitter recriminations against one another.

"To hell with it," he thought. He sat at his desk and stared at his freshly opened mail. "I'm going to ask her for a divorce. It'll never work out."

He allowed himself a measure of self-pity, reminding himself that he had married her because she was pregnant. "I'm not even certain it was mine," he said to himself. "How do I know what she was doing? She got caught, and I was available, and I'd laid her. A shotgun wedding. What can I expect? Why don't I get out?"

He tried to work through the morning, but by noon he was so restless he couldn't concentrate. Before lunch he stopped at a bar for a drink.

He never got around to lunch. At two o'clock he called his secretary and told her he had to attend to some private business and wouldn't be back. His voice was becoming thick by then. By four o'clock the bartender was politely suggesting that he had better get a cup of coffee.

Drunkenly insulted by the bartender's attitude, he had staggered from the bar and made his way to the parking lot where he had left his car. The lot attendant was hesitant about letting Tom have the car, but Tom was insistent.

He drove very slowly and with the overemphasized care that an intoxicated person may display at times. He managed to get to the outskirts of town without attracting attention from a police car.

For a while he wandered aimlessly and finally he parked in a deserted residential block in front of an empty house. He slouched down in the seat. Within a few moments he was asleep.

Even as he parked the car a jet plane took off at the airport and Altha Gateson stared with unseeing eyes out of a fuselage window. The jet passed almost directly over the man in the parked car, and its roar disturbed him vaguely so that he stirred in his drunken sleep.

"To hell with it …," he murmured. "To hell with it …"

Web Emmlin took the news of Vember's conviction with unusual calm. Quite possibly the whole thing meant the end of the Vember dealership and the Vember account in the agency. It also probably meant the termination of Web's services with the agency.

On the morning after the conviction, and like the other couples, he and Sarah read the account in the *Ledger*.

"Well, that takes care of a few things," he commented wryly.

"I'm sorry," Sarah said. "Truly, I am sorry. I know what this means at the agency, Web. Maybe there isn't much left for you and me as a married couple, but I'm not vindictive about you. I have no reason to be. And I wish you no ill luck."

"If I'm out at the agency it affects both of us," he reminded her. "There's the important matter of a pay check."

She subconsciously massaged the side of her face where she had been bruised. It was one of the small evidences of a strange preoccupation with herself, her injuries and the various scars the experience had left upon her.

"You won't have to worry about me, Web."

"I think I'll find something," he said.

"You'll still have only yourself—unless you and Agnes …" She let the sentence hang without finishing it.

"No. Not Aggie. But I'm not sure about *you* and me, Sarah. Maybe we've been mistaken. Maybe we're all wrong about this."

She shook her head. "There's no use, Web. I'm going to leave you. I can get a copywriting job somewhere. I'll make out."

"We're being too hasty."

"No. It isn't finished yet. I have to learn a great deal more about me, Web. That sounds strange, perhaps. But it's the truth. I—I've been debauched. I think that's the word. It seems as if everything has happened to me. Now I have to find out what it's all done to me—what I am."

"I'm willing to try again," he said.

She looked at him curiously. "You amaze me sometimes, Web. Truly you do. I don't understand why you still would want me. Why any man really would if he knew—"

"You're not being fair to yourself. It wasn't your fault."

"No, it wasn't my fault. But it happened. And I have to know exactly what it's done to me."

"What can you find out?" he asked. "How can you find out?"

She shrugged. "It will just have to happen. That's why I'm leaving you. I have to break free of everything, Web. I almost have to start over again."

"I can't talk you out of it?"

"No."

"All right. We have a little money in the bank. You'd beter take it. We can sell the house. You can have whatever we can get out of it, but there won't be much. We've been busy paying interest rather than principal on that loan."

"I know. I'd like to keep my car, too."

"Of course."

"Then it's really rather easy, isn't it?" she smiled.

"I don't know, Sarah. Suddenly I feel like hell about the whole thing. I wish we were starting over—just you and I."

"We've been over that. No."

"I was just telling you how I feel about it."

"What about you and Agnes?"

He looked away from her. "She's leaving the agency. A Los Angeles fashion house has offered her a job in their promotion department. She's taking it."

"I'm sorry."

He looked back at her. "Don't be sorry about *that,* Sarah. I'm the one who's sorry about that part of it. I don't know how it started up again. If it had been—well, remember the night in San Francisco? We had something that night. If it could have stayed that way …"

She remembered the night in San Francisco only too well. She knew the secret of that night, and the fantasy which somehow had made Web become Harold, her brother, for a grotesque, insane, wildly turbulent hour of released inhibitions and primitive abandon.

"Yes, I remember," she said.

Neither of them spoke, both held by their individual thoughts. Web lit a cigarette and got up to leave the breakfast table.

"So to the slaughter!" he grinned. "I wonder how they'll tell me."

"You'll find something else, Web. You're a good advertising man. Believe me, you are."

"I'm really not." He smiled, almost gently, as he looked down at her. "But thanks anyhow."

After Web had left for the agency Sarah carefully showered and dressed in a sweater and skirt. She put on dark sunglasses and went out to her car. She and Carl had made the date the day before, and she would have to hurry to be there on time.

Morning is such an unusual time for an assignation! She smiled, but without true humor. She didn't intend this to be an assignation. It was to be a meeting and a talk and one more effort to understand herself and to find out what she had become.

She drove swiftly and this time she followed the turn-off road straight to the isolated cabin. Carl's car already was there, and the door to the cabin was open. He heard her car and came out to take her in his arms at the doorway.

She let him kiss her and almost objectively she tried to ascertain what the kiss did for her, and how she felt about this man. She tried to remember how it had been before with him, and couldn't.

They went in the cabin and he closed and bolted the door.

"I wasn't certain that you'd come," he said.

"Neither was I," she said, "and that's what we said the first time we met here. Remember?"

"How could I forget?"

"Carl—I have to talk with you."

"Not yet," he said. "Something else first. You have to know that nothing's changed."

"Carl, that's one of the things I have to talk about. I'm not sure—"

He silenced her with his lips and held her hard and close until she felt her pulse quicken and the resistance began to dissolve into a familiar lassitude.

"All right," she whispered. "We'll find out."

They went into the bedroom. The morning sun flowed through the top section of a window and fell across the bed. After a while it brought out the gold in her hair and the softness of the white band of skin across her naked breasts where it contrasted with the tan. She shut her eyes and waited for his hands and lips, and when she felt them, she gasped slightly, not realizing that she would welcome them so much.

He took her in the sunlight; with gentleness and strength, so that she clung desperately to him and finally raked her nails down the broad expanse of his taut back so that in places blood came from long scratches.

Many moments later she stirred in his arms.

"Carl—was I different?" she whispered.

"You were wonderful."

"Did it change me? Am I different?" she asked again.

"More wonderful," he said softly. "More wonderful—if that could be. I love you."

"Yes—yes, you *do*, don't you, Carl!" she said, her voice affirmative in surprise.

"Yes."

After they had dressed they smoked and he told her of his plans.

"I'm taking only what I need—I can buy everything else in New York," he said rapidly. "I've talked with my attorney. I've instructed him to arrange a legal separation from Lillian. When she finds I'm never coming back, I think she'll come around to accepting divorce as the only possible solution. By that time you will have gotten your divorce from Web—and we'll be free to marry at last.

"The jet leaves tonight at midnight. I've told Lillian that I'm working late. I have your ticket. You can meet me at the airport. We'll stop in New York until we have our passports and the medical shots we may need. Then we'll take off from there. And you'll like South America—I promise you that. The firm I'm going with is excellent. The salary is high. Everything will be right for us."

"Carl—I haven't said I would. You're taking so much for granted. I can't—I can't think it out yet."

"What is there to think out?" he smiled. "It's all so logical."

CHAPTER FOURTEEN

The night was unusually hot for Douglas City. Ordinarily there was a cooling after the sun went down, but on this summer night the heat stayed over the pavement, in the apartments and homes of the downtown districts, over the lawns and fields out in the suburbs.

Windows and doors were open. Ice tinkled in cold drinks. Three-quarters of a million persons who peopled the city's metropolitan area longed for a cool marine air mass to move inland. But weather reports offered no immediate relief from the heat wave that had begun during the afternoon.

In a jail cell Len Vember felt the heat and thought about the coolness of the pool at his home. He thought of the air conditioner in his office, of long cold drinks, and he thought of Jenny Lancotte and wished that he had beaten her harder, disfigured her pretty face, broken bones!

He thought of the jail sentence to be served, and he thought of Maxine. He knew what was wrong with her—why she had mentioned divorce to him when they had been allowed to visit briefly this afternoon. It was the Gateson woman. Maxine finally had crossed the line, had embraced lesbianism. But it didn't matter—not to him, not to Len Vember. All that mattered to him was to get out.

Already—that morning—he had been taken to a room where a young man was introduced as Dr. Stein. He was a small, dark young man who wore thick glasses that seemed to intensify the intentness of his black eyes.

"Mr. Vember, I'm the police psychiatrist," he had explained.

So the new segment of life began: the sentence, the psychiatric treatment, the waiting in a cell. His lawyer had assured him that he would take care of everything on the outside and would try to get an early release. Maybe the psychiatrist could help. He'd be a willing and co-operative patient. *Anything to get out.*

Downtown, in a small, hot apartment, Jenny Lancotte watched her husband suffer. She understood his illness and the suffering and she pitied the thin, nerve-racked man who looked at her with pleading eyes of the narcotic addict too long without relief.

"Jenny … *Jenny!* I've *got* to have a fix!"

She opened a pocket book and took out two one-dollar bills. The man's empty wallet was on a table. She looked around for something to pawn. The expensive recorder already was gone. They had nothing left of any material value. He needed a fix and a fix cost money and they had only two dollars.

Abruptly she tossed her handbag and the money on the table.

"To hell with this!" she said emphatically. "We lost our mark. I took a beating. We haven't any loot. You need a fix. There's only one answer."

The man watched her. His agony of need was deeply etched in his face and movements.

Jenny went to a telephone and dialed. A woman's voice answered.

"Miranda?" Jenny said.

"Jenny! Where have you been?"

"Around. It's been a long time. I didn't know if you'd still have the same number."

"I've been lucky," the woman laughed softly. "Are you working?"

"No. That's why I called. I need money. Can you use me?"

"You're all right? I mean, I saw the papers. You look all right? He didn't hurt you too bad?"

"No. I'm fine, Miranda. He slapped me around mostly."

"That was a big deal, honey. You can tell me about it sometime."

"Sure. But how about now, Miranda? Tonight? Can you use me?"

"There's a fifty-dollar trick down at a hotel. He just called. A regular from out of town. Interested?"

"Yes. Give me the rest."

When she hung up, the man watched her with the same suffering look, and now tears were in his eyes.

"I didn't want this to happen, baby," he whispered. "I wanted to keep you out of the life."

"It's all right," she said, almost soothingly. She knew—God, how she knew—what he was going through! She'd been there.

She went into the bedroom and undressed. She took a quick bath and dressed again with fresh panties, bra and a black slip under her dark summer frock. She wished the heat would let up. She wondered why men still wanted sex on a hot, uncomfortable, sticky night.

Before she left the room she checked herself in a mirror. She scrutinized her face as if she might be looking at a stranger, and then her smile came, slightly crooked and bitterly amused.

"Once a call girl, always a call girl," she said to herself.

She went out into the living room and kissed the man before she left.

"Miranda said she'd send twenty by taxi," she told him. "You can get your fix. I'll be back—when I'm finished. Maranda thinks I may have a couple of calls."

As she went down in the automatic elevator she wondered if the *Ledger* would investigate prostitution for its series on crime.

Five miles away at the city's new, mammoth airport Sarah Emmlin and Carl Trojan stood by a gate in one of the concourses. Passengers already had gone out to the waiting jet.

"Change your mind, Sarah," Carl said. "Follow me tomorrow—or I'll wait."

"No, Carl. I came out here to say good-by. And that's it. Maybe in weeks … months … a year … I'll feel different. But not now. I can't go with you. I don't love you that much."

He looked at her with unhappy eyes, but with the calm acceptance that he had displayed when she had arrived at the airport and told him of her decision.

"If you don't love me enough, I guess that's answer enough for now," he said, as if he was making a logical decision based upon formula. "But I'm going, Sarah. Maybe that's why I can't fight you too much on your decision. I know how it is to have to get away. So I'm going. But I want you—at any price. Follow me. I'll be at the Waldorf in New York. Call me there if you change your mind."

"I won't."

He studied her and nodded. He touched her cheek with a hand and kissed her on the mouth.

"Good-by, Sarah," he said.

She smiled without speaking. She watched him walk through the gateway, past the attendent checking passengers and out to the jet. At the door into the airplane he turned and waved, then he was gone.

Sarah walked back along the concourse toward an escalator. She rode up into the large waiting room and walked quickly toward exits to the parking lots.

Someone touched her shoulder. She looked back and Web was there.

He said, "I saw you go down with Carl. I thought you might be running away with him. It gave me a hell of a start!"

"I changed my mind," she said frankly. "He wanted me to go."

He shook his head in a gesture of despair at his own lack of discernment. "I didn't know there was anything between you two. I guess there's been a lot I didn't know."

"It only started a little while ago," she said. "You've been too busy with Agnes to notice."

He smiled ruefully and didn't answer. They walked toward the parking lots.

"You didn't call," she said. "I mean about the agency. What happened?"

"Vember is selling out to his sales manager and some others. They want us to keep the account—changing the dealership name. I'm still working."

"I'm glad, Web."

"I came out to see Agnes off to L.A. So I guess we've taken care of most of the loose ends—the major ones, that is."

"Yes."

They were at the parking area.

"We both have cars. Are you going to the house?"

"For tonight. I'm glad I ran into you. If you're not going straight home, may I borrow your key? I left mine in another bag."

"I'm going to stop for a drink. You'll probably be there first."

He took out a key case and unsnapped his house key. He held it out to her and as she took it their eyes locked. Obviously the same thought had crossed their minds.

He spoke: "In a corny TV half-hour drama they'd probably end the picture here with a tag line about the key—and the key game. Probably with a line like 'This is where we came in ' "

"Or where we went out," she smiled.

"But this isn't a corny TV drama," he said.

"That's right, Web."

"There's no use making a pitch? I want us together again."

"No use, Web. At least not yet. Maybe sometime. I still have to find out what's happened to me."

"Sure," he said. "Sure, I understand."

"I'll leave the key under the mat—in case you're late."

"I don't suppose you'd have a drink with me?"

"No, Web. No … to everything."

"That's what I thought."

She left him and walked along a row of cars until she found hers. A jet roared in take-off into the summer night. She didn't look up. She got in her car and for a long time she sat there without starting the engine nor turning on the lights.

Abruptly, but not violently, she began to weep. The tears rolled unheeded down her cheeks and fell into her lap.

"I'm so alone … so *damned alone …*" she sobbed.…

After a while she wiped the tears from her eyes and face and started the car. She drove home and when she arrived Web's car was in the driveway. He was sitting on the front doorstep, smoking.

"I came straight home," he said. "I've been waiting—no key."

"I'm glad," she said.

"Glad?"

Suddenly she no longer felt so alone. She still didn't know what she was going to do, but for some unexplained reason she *was* glad that he had come straight home and was waiting.

"Glad that you're waiting," she said and handed him his key.

THE END